There's a place that's far away
an' a little mound of clay
That recalls to me the days of long ago
When I set on Mother's knee
An' she talked and sang to me
How I loved her voice an' accent sweet an' low
Oh her love will always linger
I can see her day by day
As she sat there in that little cabin home
Tho' the house is gone away
An' the fields with grass are gray
I can n'er forget my Ozark mountain home

George Edgin's Corn Dodgers
"My Ozark Mountain Home"

RELEASE THE HORSE
Copyright © 2025 by Matthew Mitchell

This is a work of fiction. Names, characters, businesses, places, events, locales, and incidents are either the products of the author's imagination or used in a fictitious manner. Any resemblance to actual persons, living or dead, or actual events is purely coincidental.

This book may not be reproduced in whole or in part, except for the inclusion of brief quotations in a review, without permission in writing from the author or publisher. No part of this publication may be reproduced, stored in or introduced into retrieval system, or transmitted, in any form, or by any means (electronic, mechanical, photocopying, recording, or otherwise), without prior permission of the publisher.

Requests for permission should be directed to

filthylootpress@gmail.com

"Matthew Mitchell's stories exist at the intersection of campfire tale, unchronicled ancestral folklore, and a Weird cosmology that's irrefutably his own. His gift of gab keeps you firmly in his thrall, whether he's piercing your heart or turning your stomach; you'll be grinning at his witty turns of phrase as the sun sinks beneath the hills and the Woolybugger creeps up behind you."

—**Madison McSweeney** (Author, *Most Likely to Summon Nyhiloteph, The Doom That Came to Mellonville*)

"There's sweat and grime and dirt and blood in every word of Matthew Mitchell's short fiction collection. Fight Club monks and sexy ass worm women and Big Babies and older things and the protagonists of these stories don't seem like they have any chance of survival. This is a violent world whose inhabitants live in the shadow of violent men. But you can tell that Matthew wants them to survive. Wants them to live and thrive despite all the toxicity and the hurt. And in that sincerity, in Matthew's empathy for his characters, is where the book shines. I, for one, gained ten pounds of muscle just by reading this book and I ain't ever going back. So, join me and rejoice in Matthew's words. Join the Church of Daniel, you cowards."

— **Xavier Garcia** (short fiction writer & editor at *Twin Pies Literary*)

"These are the stories your drunk cousin tells you around a bonfire when you were too young to hear them. The ones you never forget. What Matthew Mitchell offers us is rural communion, the flesh and blood of strange happenings that occur in Nowhere, USA. Weird and surreal, for sure, but so very close to the homegrown folk tales passed down through oral traditions. Real and the grotesque are thinly veiled and it makes it so much more disturbing when the stories are finished."

— **Edwin Callihan** (author, *Strange Spells*)

YARNS OF RURAL ODDITY

RELEASE THE HORSE

MATTHEW MITCHELL

Filthy Loot

RELEASE THE HORSE

There's a lot of folks who know about the horse, but I reckon there ain't many who care to see it. I've heard it said that the thing is enough to make a man sick. They say ol' Miller Calhoun never should've made it in the first place—say it ain't right. Ungodly, and such.

I myself have seen the horse on many occasions. Don't bother me, so long as I don't look it in the eye. Fact is, I sort of like watching it run. Makes me feel like there's still some magic left to the world. Not saying it's a pretty sight or nothing. Not like I'd roll my Momma out there for a picnic. But if'n I'm bored enough—if the right mood strikes—I'll take the walk to Calhoun's place and take in the sights.

So it goes that last Tuesday, I was in need of an escape.

See, my roommate ain't what you'd call a personable sort, and our trailer don't got room enough to piss without stumbling over one another. Worse yet, he keeps a woman around, and she don't do much for his disposition. They fuck like snakes on warm limestone—a raucous affair that shakes our little tin-trap something fierce. She likes to walk around nekkid, or half so and gives me the look whenever she gets a chance. I ain't one to turn down a free show or a quick pump, but her man's not the type I'd care to tussle with. He bats her around pretty good once they get going. All that hollering and smacking makes me nervous.

She don't seem to mind. Says she likes it when Daddy lays her out good. Told me so her own damn self. Fact of the matter is, I believe it. It's a bad scene. Disgusting, really, and I can't abide it long 'til I get itching to leave. Got to go someplace else.

Somewhere quiet.

That's about the skinny as to how I found myself leaning on the rail down at Calhoun's farm. I was looking out at his clapboard shack—at the mildewed barn that sat a few paces off—smoking hand rolls and waiting. It was soon-to-dark, and I knew the crazy coot didn't release the horse 'fore night come. Never was sure if that was part of how it worked, you know? Weren't a full-moon or nothing, last time I seen it. Don't reckon it would blow away to ash come sunup.

Didn't take it for no monster.

Figure maybe Calhoun just had sense enough to keep the horse in the dark so's nobody would see. Might be right. Don't seem like the sort of thing you'd want your kids to come across. That there's a highway to questions without answers and dreams with shining eyes. But like I say, I ain't faint hearted—'cept maybe when it comes to matters of domestic savagery.

Anyhow, I weren't out there long 'til I seen my roommate and his woman coming up the dirt road. She had a sliced-up pair of jean shorts hauled over her nekkid ass and nothing else. He was much the same: Big, flat feet wedged into boots—topped off

RELEASE THE HORSE

with a filthy pair of boxers—and his dead paw's Stetson on his head. Both of them wore cloaks of scabs and bruised flesh—wardrobe of their sickness.

I hoped to God they'd keep on. Prayed they was headed up to Big Booger's for a beer. I could tell they been riding the lightbulb by the way she scratched at her open sores—by the rigid meanness set across his jaw.

Sure as shit, I watched him palm the pipe to his woman as they come up on me. She stumbled to a halt and torched the bulb—gave it a good, rough pull. I could smell the smoke 'fore I seen it bubble between her lips: cat piss and charred corn chips—the hometown special.

My roommate must've spotted me standing there at the pasture gate, grabbed her by the elbow, and stalked over to me. She offered the lightbulb with spastic hands. It burned my fingers when I took it—boiled my throat as I puffed.

"What y'all doing here?" I asked.

"We come to fuck," he answered.

"A roll in the hay," she said and laughed.

He whacked her across the tit and pulled at

a pale nipple. "You want it?" he asked me. "Five bucks or some grass."

"Yeah," she said—reached around his mighty grip searched for my crotch. "Let's have us a party."

He let go of her breast and slugged the back of her head with an open palm. "The Hell you say?"

"Ow, Daddy," she groaned. "I was only foolin'."

"Damn right," he said—pulled at her long, dirty hair. "The fuck're you doing out here?" He stared me down as his woman snaked her hand through his cotton fly.

I guess the lightbulb hit done me good on account of my reply: "I'm doing my damndest to get away from y'all."

His muscled brow tightened in the gloom. "That right?"

"Sure is," I replied. "Heard enough of your humpin' to last me two lifetimes and a ticket to Jesus."

"Thump him, Daddy," she said.

He turned her loose and made a go at me, so I busted the bulb against the fence and jabbed for his face. That stopped him—put his arms back by his sides, kept his distance. Might have been figuring out his next move, but then came the slap of a screen door from down pasture, and we all turned to look.

Miller Calhoun had come out his shack and made a beeline for the old barn. He was bare-backed beneath his oily bibs and muttered up a storm. His white hair went wild in the dusky breeze—a thick silver key dangled from his fist.

"Oh," my roommate said. "I get it. You come out here to see that fuckin' horse."

I declined to respond, and so his woman asked: "What whore? Ol' Calhoun runnin' pussy? Wouldn't peg him for pimpin'. How many whores has he got?"

"Horse, goddamn you. I said horse."

"Oh, well, shit! I just love a horse. Why ain't we got us a horsey, Daddy? What kind of horse you say it was?"

"You'll see." He put a ruddy finger against his woman's mouth to dam her druggish babble. "You're gonna love this." A wet smile etched over his chin. "Won't she, buddy-boy?" He stretched out and pushed my shoulder with his fingertips—kept his eyes on the broken bulb.

'Fore another word passed between us, Calhoun got his key through the latch. The barn door swung open with a scream. There was a loud snort from inside, and the old man said something as if in reply. He stepped back.

Out come the horse.

Hard to say what you compare it to. A kid's equine rendition through a clump of clay? No, that ain't right. Had more intent to it than that from the hands of a child. The perversity of the horse felt earned. Crafted. Designed by dragons or devils. Is there a difference? Guess I don't know.

"Bet it ain't even real." My roommate hocked up a gobber—spat into the pasture. "Cain't be."

"Say, Mister," his woman called out to Calhoun: "What type of horsey you got there? Looks sick or something."

The old man got up onto his tilted porch and yelled back: "You all keep away. It don't matter what the county says, that there horse is mine." He put a hand to his lips beneath the heavenly body. "Made it with my own two hands. Built from mud, teeth, tubers—whatever I could find. I seen it in my sleep. Don't run for nobody but me. I don't got to tell y'all a goddamn thing . . ."

He kept on like that for a while, but we quit hearing it. The horse had come up alongside the gate—real close like—and it was hard to look away. Captivated by the strangeness of it. Transfixed, you might say. Calhoun must have known we was a lost cause—heard the screen flap shut to his shack and nothing more.

"Will you just look at it," I said. "Dear God almighty."

My roommate—fool that he was—passed his prized Stetson to his woman and bounded over the gate. "Watch this shit," he said, and charged the horse.

It faced him directly and watched his approach with stoic, marble eyes. Never even flinched.

The dumb bastard grabbed the horse by its row of spinal mane—hand to bone—and made to pull himself over. As his leg came up against the horse's side, it swiveled its wide head and opened its mouth.

He yelped in pain—let go of the horse. Blood sprang from his chest, and he turned to run. He looked at us through the fence, and the horse snatched up a fleshy sheet from his back. On twisted ankles, he fell.

The horse dipped back down for another bite.

He started to cry—wept like a suckling brat.

That got his woman laughing. There weren't much to her—starved from food, gorged on dust—but I reckon you would call it a real belly-shaker. She laughed so hard I seen the tears twinkle in her eyes by the light of a half moon.

"You done it now, Daddy," she said. "Boy, is he in Dutch."

The horse kept at him as she cackled, and me just watching. After a time, his screams cut out—gave way to the sound of crunching. Gnawing.

Square teeth on wet grass.

His woman shushed up and dried her eyes with the back of her hand. She placed the Stetson atop her head and with the lithe grace of a creekbed panther, vaulted the fence—landed on the horse where it fed. It reared back once, and she grabbed its spine with one hand—threw back the other, high above her hat.

For a moment, just a moment, she was a rodeo God set against the black velvet of night. Her scabs fell away, and her hair turned to spinning gold. The horse took off with her astride. Arched of back, fair of pallor. I seen her and the horse ride away together through the field of stars.

Sure was quiet when I got back to the trailer. Had the whole can to myself. Real nice, tell you what. Been that a'way ever since.

But I do tend to wonder if ol' Calhoun ever seen that horse again. I ain't been by in some time and don't reckon I will.

MUSCULAR DEVOTION

The churchhouse was quaint and smelled of hickory smoke; six rows of seats bordering a cherrywood aisle that shined like glass. Upon the floor were massive, muddy footprints left by the preacher—trailed by Dean's smaller steps—which ran from the front door to the altar where they stood.

"Welcome, brother," the preacher said and bowed his bald pate. He reached out and gripped Dean's upper arms.

The two men were covered from beard to toe in drying clay and blood. Naked, save the earth which coated their bodies. Eyes and teeth, white like the winter sun.

RELEASE THE HORSE

"You fight with courage," the preacher said. "Our flock needs men like you."

"I'm honored, Father Lisle."

"Brother Lisle." The preacher corrected him. "He who walks among us is a peer in blood."

The preacher's grip deadened a nerve in Dean's neck. It would be weak of him to flinch or flex. He resisted the urge and nodded.

"For men of your strength and devotion, there is but one Father." They both looked to the rafters. "And He sees you for what you are: a warrior of God, master of all but that which whirls above our heads. This is what you have earned." The preacher released him.

Nerve unclamped, Dean's blood flowed freely. Relief flooded tender veins, and his jaw unclenched.

"You are one of us." Brother Lisle spread his arms—swollen with muscle—and dried earth fell from him to shatter on the floor. The preacher let his head tip back onto his shoulders. "You are an angel," he said. "An angel without wings."

A tear rolled down Dean's cheek. The droplet drifted through mud and welled within a nail-shaped wound. It burned him.

Dean also sported a broken rib—that was certain—but the sanctity of his left kidney soon came into question.

Their fight in the churchyard—Dean's initiation—had been brutal. The preacher packed in more body-shots than he ever would have expected for a man of his age. Hard, intrusive wallops that moved things around on the inside. The two loose jabs to his temple were nothing to shrug at either.

Brother Lisle was easily the largest and most imposing human being he ever laid eyes upon. And there had been many, many large men in Dean's life. But none of them compared to the preacher's magnitude or viciousness, let alone pushing-seventy with the liver spots and wrinkles to prove it.

Size, it would seem, still counted for something.

Size and faith, he decided.

Dean himself was not a man of any great stature. Just under six foot, average shoulders, and muscle, which was earned if not well-defined. Hard living had created the strength within Dean's humble frame, not weight machines or dutiful hours in a gym. He had learned to fight through a cruel childhood and the self-imposed depravity of his twenties. Violence as a chosen path. An eternal facet to his broken life…Until he walked into the Church of Daniel for the first time.

Until he found God.

"I'm sorry—" Dean looked down at the filthy mass of hair and meat between his legs.

His thoughts returned to their combat: the mud squelching beneath his toes inside the fighting-pen, punches and kicks and scrapings. The way his penis had throbbed as the preacher pressed against him, the triumphant splatter he let loose as his soiled opponent twisted and writhed within his grasp.

" —I didn't mean to do that."

"Now, now," the preacher said. His pendulous arms fell to Dean's waist and held him by the hips.

Brother Lisle forced Dean's shameful eyes to meet his own; met them with love and understanding.

"God made men in His image. Our lusts, our

affection," he pressed his wrinkled forehead into Dean's, "they are His as well as ours. These rods of desire given to us by His Majesty—" the preacher's hand traced the length of Dean's thigh "—these are a reflection of strength. The hardness of our faith."

Dean sighed, and breath whistled between teeth. His armpits dampened. Soft flutters.

"Do not be ashamed of what we are, Brother Dean." The preacher relinquished his grasp. He cracked their skulls together in a mighty headbutt and laughed a low, joyous bellow. "What's a little cum upon the battlefield in the eyes of God?"

Like familiar echoes in a jailhouse weight room, Dean found comfort in the holy man's manner of speaking. His ability to flit between profound proclamations of the Lord God, so familiar, the brashness of a commoner's tongue, just like coming home.

The preacher sat down on the altar steps. A light wheeze emitted from his bruised throat, and his knees cracked.

"When will I meet the others—?" Dean stammered, "—my brothers, I mean."

"Our brothers are on a hunt."

"Oh."

"We stalk the eastern hills with knives and bodies bare. Devotion to the temple of muscle as our only shields." The preacher inspected a gash on his left heel; a stone from the churchyard muck was embedded in the wound. "Wild boar roam these thickets through February. A worthy adversary, if ever there was one. Cloven-hooved monsters born from the loose lips of Satan." Brother Lisle shucked the rock free from his calloused foot and put it in his mouth.

Dean shivered. He imagined the weight of a tusk popping naked skin. Miles and miles of snow needling into heels.

Yes, he thought, I need this.

"If I left now, could I catch up?" Dean asked.

Brother Lisle looked up at him. He sucked the stone and plucked it from his lips. "By the thorns of Jesus," he said, "you are a wonder." His lips cascaded into a heartworn smile. "No, not tonight. They'll be back before we know it." He stood on jittering ankles. "Why don't we take a tour of the

Lion's Den?"

The preacher led Dean through a nondescript door behind the altar. A staircase— hewn from the same bright cherrywood as the church house floor—took them two stories beneath the grounds.

Unlike the church above, this room was immense. A square, concrete chamber, brightly lit by dozens of halogen tube lights. In the center of the room, a twelve-foot wooden cross cast quadruple shadows on the floor.

The left half of the space housed several makeshift barbells and weights: anvils welded to iron poles, steel kegs with bloodied cloth strapped to the handles…A throne-bearing monstrosity of rebar and rusted pulleys which resembled an enormous crossbow.

Dean's mouth watered.

"This—" Brother Lisle twirled beneath the cross, arms wide, palms open "—is our domain."

The other half of the chamber was divided into four quadrants: at the back of the room, a series of gun racks had been bolted to the wall and housed an array of semi-automatic rifles, pistols, and shotguns.

A pegboard panel in the next space was laden with white ski masks, kidskin work gloves, and hangers bearing eggshell coveralls. Beside this, a case of handwrought bowie knives; each piece of identical blade length and bone-hewn handle.

Dean stood before the final quadrant: a large opening in the concrete wall. Not quite a doorway, but more calculated in its design than a simple hole. The opening was surrounded by a lead gate which graced the ceiling with its highest hinges. The gate appeared to be very old, and a heavy latch sealed it shut.

Greenish foam trickled out from the black chasm, and the sound of rushing wind came forth like the tail-end of a freight train.

"What's in there?" Dean asked.

"Brother Daniel," the preacher replied.

Dean waited, but Brother Lisle did not elaborate.

Instead, the naked preacher drifted down to the weapon racks and fatigues. He plucked a ski mask from its peg and pulled it over his face. There was a black crucifix stitched upon the forehead, and it reminded Dean of a cranial wound or prison tattoos—much like the ones which covered his own nude body.

"The Church of Daniel is on a mission—" the preacher began.

"To kill the boar," Dean interrupted.

Brother Lisle's pupils widened to black orbs. The balaclava exacerbated this effect and bestowed the preacher with an affected look of some putrid deepwater shark.

"Sorry," Dean said. His face burned with shame.

"There are greater wars on God's earth than hunting wretched swine," the preacher said. His eyes softened as he lifted a twelve gauge from its rack. "Devils take many forms, Brother Dean. They walk on more than cloven hooves, I can assure you. And though their teeth may not be tusked like their screw-tailed brethren," Brother Lisle smiled, "they bite just as hard."

Dean held his breath.

Would he say it? Was the preacher going to tell him about the bodies found buried beneath

Cooper's Hill? Would he explain the massacre at Oak Shade Methodist? Or the dead kids at the mainstreet protest—?

"When the time comes," Brother Lisle pumped the shotgun, "you'll learn our rules of engagement. The ways of holy terror."

Dean exhaled.

"If you do wrong, be afraid. For warriors do not bear the sword for no reason," Brother Lisle recited. "They are God's soldiers of wrath to bring punishment."

"Romans-thirteen," Dean said. He bowed his head before the shotgun barrel.

"Warriors hold no terror," Brother Lisle continued. "Does thou wish to be free from fear?"

"I do."

"Good. Tomorrow night, you will join us as we thrust our swords upon—"

The door to the stairway burst open above them. A stampede of hard feet. Gruff voices speaking low and fast. Among them, someone was crying. Screaming.

To Dean's attuned ears, it sounded like the pain of death at one's door.

Before he and Brother Lisle could exchange glances, a herd of nude men came flying into the chamber. There were nine in total, and they moved in a circle—some scuttling sideways or backward—with a bloodied man held aloft between them. The man's hands were clamped to his side, a pink ribbon of intestine looped over his thumb. He bawled as his bearers kneeled to lay him beside the wooden cross.

There was red around his mouth and ears.

"Brother Jasper," the preacher said. He pushed the shotgun into Dean's arms and fell to the wounded man on cracking knees. "What the fuck—?"

"Ol' Scratch got him," a man with a thick mustache answered. He rubbed his meaty shoulders, skin nearly blue from exposure. "We missed. Again." He hung his head, tendrils of his curly mullet dripping melted snow and sweat.

"No," the preacher smashed his fist against the concrete floor. "Don't call it that."

RELEASE THE HORSE

"Yes, Brother Lisle," the mullet-man replied.

"A demon," Brother Jasper croaked. He began to sputter and choked on a sob. A gout of purple blood whizzed from between his teeth.

"Hush now," Brother Lisle said. He caressed Jasper's face, and his fingers smeared blood across the pale brow like a child's painting. "Just a pig, that's all. Tremble not, Brother, and let the bosom of His Majesty comfort you in this time of–"

"Aint—" Brother Jasper coughed, "—no pig. Demon. Demon. Demon—"

"What do we do, Father?" A fat man with pierced nipples asked. There was a tattoo of Jesus' face on his enormous belly, a surgical scar beneath the navel.

"I'm not your father, Brother Kevin."

"My apologies, Brother—"

"What the fuck are we gonna do, Lisle?" The man with the mullet stepped up. His shadow fell over the preacher and his mortally wounded charge. "We ain't going to no hospital. Ain't no doctors here. A boar in the guise of man walks the field yonder and wishes us dead. So we ask again: what are you gonna do about it?"

Dean saw violence spread across the mullet-man's face like a bruise. Somebody was going to get hurt. Someone besides poor Brother Jasper, who still clung to life by a thread of fear.

Dean had seen men die like this before. He knew there was no religion in that kind of suffering. Bargains with older, rarer Gods took place in those loathsome deaths.

"He'll be alright," the preacher said. "Don you nothing but the full armor of God, and thou can stand against the monsters of Satan—"

Dean paced across the room, dropped to one knee, and raised the shotgun.

"Wait," Brother Lisle reached for the barrel.

The Brothers of Daniel leapt away or else stared on, confused and rattled.

"Mercy," Dean said as he pulled the trigger.

Brother Jasper's head erupted against the base of the cross. His skull—cleaved in two—collapsed and shriveled like a flower-bud of flesh and bone. Blood splattered throughout the chamber; little flecks of lost life in every corner, on every surface.

No one could hear anything for a long time, but everyone spoke or shouted. Everyone but Dean. He sat down, and his naked buttocks instantly chaffed on the rugged floor. The mullet man shouted in his face but his ears had not stopped ringing. He nodded in silence and waited for the lost sense to return. Warm fluid drifted lazily from Brother Jasper's corpse to pool around his thigh.

It was the warmest Dean had felt all day.

"—has to pay for this," he heard, like a voice from above the water's surface.

"That animal out there," Brother Lisle said, "that's the beast that deserves our scorn. Not him." The preacher pointed at Dean. "Do not seek vengeance from He who is among your flock."

"Where'd you hear that one, Lisle?" The mullet man said. "'Fraid I don't recall that particular sermon." He and three others hovered to his left.

The fat one—Brother Kevin—stared at Dean with his teeth bared.

"Did I not hear you call that boar by the name of Satan himself? Is it not your claim that Brother

Jasper was taken from us by his infernal tusk? What say you then, Brother Jim?"

"I said he was gored by the beast yonder," Brother Jim pointed to the staircase, mullet-tail flapping. "We all seen the hand that took Brother Jasper's life. And before God's holy cross, no less."

"When one of our Brothers fall, another must be ushered in." The preacher stood and bent down to snatch the shotgun away.

Dean had forgotten he still clung to it.

"We brought this man in after what happened to—"

"Don't you dare say his name, old man. That snake sought to speak of what we done. The holy stand at Cooper's Hill. Those fucking kids and their little handmade signs. He called the law, dammit. Remember that? He weren't one of us." Brother Jim spat crossed his arms.

"Be that as it may—" Brother Lisle passed the twelve gauge to a naked man who now stood behind him. "—this man before you is your Brother. He fought hard and made his affections known to me. He is one of us, an angel of the earth, and we do not take arms against our own. This shall not stand."

Lines have been drawn, Dean thought.

The chamber fell silent. Brother Jim and his men bristled. One stepped forward beside his mulleted comrade. Brother Kevin shuffled his bulk and uncurled his thick arms. Furtive movements of the bloodshed about to erupt.

"Brother Daniel is here," someone said.

All eyes turned to the large opening in the corner of the room. Some of the men gasped while others stepped swiftly aside. Brother Lisle padded over to the gate and wrapped his fists around the bars.

It took Dean several moments to decipher what he saw standing in front of the chasm, behind the rusted gate.

An eight foot man-thing. A bullet head and small features that were swallowed entirely by the proportions of its body. Muscle tightly woven, delicately placed, outward and upon itself, like a braided leather belt. Alien, alarming, and unnatural. Six-packs where they should not be, and which spanned the length of it, from armpit to armpit. The arms of Daniel– this thing – hovered at its side as both were too swollen with bubbled tissue to truly come to rest against equally distended ribs.

Daniel's heavy breathing was the source, Dean discovered, of that blasphemous wheezing he had heard coming from the blackness.

"Hello, Brother Daniel," the preacher said. He clicked his tongue and cooed. "My sweet boy."

Brother Daniel stared back at the preacher with the eyes of an idiot. Brown drool trickled over his tiny lips and he shifted his snow shovel feet. He was nude, wrapped in the fleshy armor of God, as were all in the chamber.

The club-shaped organ between its thighs was blistered and weeping.

"What in God's name," Dean said. He stood and pressed his back to the cross. Cold sweat oozed from his pores. His heel slipped on Brother Jasper's blood and he went down again. He hugged his knees with both arms where he sat.

"This is your Brother," the preacher whirled on

him. "The culmination of our divine efforts. The Lord God sent us his strongest, purest angel to aid us in our mission."

Dean looked the man-thing up and down: a calamitous and impossible illustration of a comic book champion, perhaps. But a deitous creature sent from the heavens?

He thought not.

Brother Daniel's attention was drawn to Dean. Those slow moving eyes tracked him as he shivered and rocked himself. The goliath began to shake the bars. Brother Lisle stepped back.

"Give him to Brother Daniel," someone said.

"Yeah," Brother Jim agreed. "Brother Daniel wants him."

The cage moaned as Brother Daniel throttled his bars. Bits of concrete fell to the floor where the top hinges scraped against the ceiling. Brother Daniel's member swayed and slapped against his legs from the force of his efforts. The sound of steel on stone and pounding meat filled the chamber.

"Wait a minute," Brother Lisle said. "Just wait a damn minute." The preacher moved his body in front of Dean like a shield.

"Brother Daniel has needs," Brother Jim said. "He wants to show us his strength. Let him give his affections to his new Brother."

"He isn't ready."

"Fuck this." Brother Jim stalked his way over to the gate. His mullet was dotted with blood and bits of Brother Jasper's skull.

Brother Kevin waddled up to the other side of the bars. The two usurpers exchanged grins and heaved open the latch.

Brother Daniel had not taken his bird eyes off of Dean. As the latch clicked, the giant shouldered the bars and pushed free from the enclosure. Brother Kevin and Brother Jasper were thrown sideways, onto the floor.

The preacher stepped back. "Daniel," he said, "listen to me. This is Dean... your Brother. Please–" he pleaded "–be sweet to him. Not like the others."

Dean rose behind the preacher. He cracked his neck and squared his shoulders. He brushed Brother Lisle aside.

"I'm ready," he said.

Brother Daniel seemed to consider this before reaching out to grip the wooden cross from above Dean's head. The crucifix shucked free from its concrete wedge and splinters the size of pencils cascaded like pine needles. The goliath gripped the cross by the crux; wielded it inverted, like a sword, and let loose a rancid scream from the back of its throat.

Dean wiped the snot from his face, and raised both fists to his ears. "By the strength of God," he said.

The giant swung his cross and Dean tried not to flinch.

BIG BABY

Swore I'd get gone 'fore dark. An early morning promise I made and forgot. And by the time I heard the first night-hawk, I knew I'd fuckered myself.

Still had my line out, kept getting tugged, and I refused to let go. Something playing grab-ass with my bait; we'd been doing the dance for an hour with no end in sight. A haul worth hanging around for.

Once upon a time, I'd have brung my blacklight rig down here by the shore. Pick me up a box of crickets, a spool of glow-line…

Not no more.

Night-fishing was off the table; had been ever since them folks started turning up dead. All fish and game activities been banned after dark til further notice. That's directly from the Sheriff's Office.

Not that I'd abide orders from town-dwelling hogs, mind you.

Fact of the matter is, we ain't even supposed to cast down this end of the river. That there is a decree by souls who wander deeper woods than me. An old-timey pact among true and blue locals. Conservation efforts, they like to say.

I figure maybe I was feeling bold on account of the whopper at hand. I'd started upstream but followed the bites all the way down. Pole dipping and slicing the whole way. My bait stock weren't long for this world by then, so I guess I just kept at it.

And besides, there ain't been a Big Baby sighting in…Hell, three years? Personally, I ain't seen it since I's a kid. It don't worry me much. Never did.

Even so, I played it purty safe down there. You just stick to worms or shad, and Big Baby won't bother you none. Sure, I'm tempted to hunt channel-cats on a warm evening', but I know better than to dip into my stinkbait. Not in these parts.

That ain't got nothing to do with why I weren't keen on the diving sun. Cus, like I say, local pigs don't scare me. Wildlife neither.

See, I was concerned about an outsider who'd claimed the lives of four– no– five hikers this past season. Beat to death, hacked to pieces, strewn about the trees. Grisly stuff.

Murderer on the loose or not, I had me a fish to catch. Wasn't about to let this fucker tease me and just walk away. Any bass stalker worth their weight'll tell you the same: a good haul is a good haul, daylight be damned.

I'll spare you the sorrow of my efforts. We'll say I sunk the hook, gave it the good fight and snapped the line just as I pulled to shore. Won't say how close. Won't lie as to the size. I ain't here to tell no stories.

Only the truth.

I reeled in, line broke and weightless, just cussin' up a storm…And I hear this voice behind me.

"A dirty shame," they said.

RELEASE THE HORSE

Boy, I nearly jumped clear out my britches. It weren't just the fact someone crept up on me without so much as a twig-snap. Nor the closeness which they had obtained. It was the way they said it: the coldness of it.

My Daddy taught me it's best not to let a threat know you've been affected. Let 'em think you've kept your cucumber cool, even if they seen your hackles raise. Much as my head wanted to turn and face my visitor, I kept both eyes on the water and reeled in my dead line.

"Looked like a big one."

I heard 'em approach down the bank. Heavy steps on loose pebble. They wasn't trying to hide no more than a wasp in June.

"Uh-huh," I mustered.

"Hate to see it," they said.

My line came up out the river and into the pole. I tied it off in a bunny-ear and knelt beside my tackle box. Took a deep breath, wished I had a smoke. Down there on one knee, I tilted my eyes ever so slightly...

I seen the buck-knife first. A fat, nasty wedge

of silver in a gloved fist. The knife burned bright white in the fading sun. There was a camo ski mask pulled over their face. Eyes obscured by a pair of thick glasses.

Jesus, I thought, this how it ends?

I was about to jump to my feet— thought I'd swing my rod, try to catch this punk's face with a good switch or two, 'fore— well, you know…

But then I heard the branch snap.

Sounded more like the trunk of a tree, if'n I'm being honest. I weren't the only one who heard it neither; the masked stranger flipped around so fast I thought they'd put out their neck.

Big Baby stood beside a wide oak, watching us.

Now, like I say, hadn't seen it in years, but I knew what I was looking at. Even with the sun now gone and it standing beneath a wealth of black shade, I could see the burst of hair, them yellow eyes…the size of it.

Smelled like burnin' squirrel fur and rotten fish.

The stranger must've seen it, too, or sniffed it out at least. They started backin' up towards me, makin' little noises in their throat. Head low, knees bent, they waved the knife back and forth like a motorboat.

Big Baby stepped out from the trees and onto the bank with feet as flat and long as swamp lilies. The odor swelled. It swiped at the outsider– half-hearted– and whined like a child.

Don't know what compelled me to do what I done next, but I ducked beside my tackle and fished around until I found the jar. I opened the bottle of B.J.'s stinkbait and dipped my hand into the mush. It stunk so bad— like it's supposed to— that it nearly drowned out Big Baby's inimitable funk.

The outsider backed into me, shucking that blade around. Had to duck the knife to keep my nose.

I hopped up, real close, and smeared that stinkbait all over the back of their head.

The B.J. clung to the mask like wet shit, and I hauled out the rest to slather it down their shoulders. The stranger jerked around and took a stab at my face. I sidestepped off the bank and threw myself backward into the water.

Big Baby come up alongside them.

It sniffed at the air.

I watched it grab that masked sucker by the arm and wrench it off with a pop.

Made it look easy.

The knife fell, and they might've screamed, but Big Baby picked them up by the waist and stuffed their head inside its mouth.

I closed my eyes but still heard the crunch. Kinda like a ripe melon under a boot. There was a sloshin' sound, too. No screams, though.

Just noises.

I wonder what it is makes a thing like Big Baby go crazy for stinkbait. The chicken gullet? Aged blood? Must be the perfect mix.

Anyhow, I swam, fast as I could, got clear to the other bank, and didn't look back.

Them murders stopped after that. And I feel bad not reporting to the pigs. Families of them dead folks deserve their peace. But I kept my trap shut.

RELEASE THE HORSE

Wouldn't want no game wardens coming through here. They might could find Big Baby. I figure they'd consider it a threat, beast like that.

We can't have it.

We protect our own 'round here.

Next time I go down to the river— not sure when that'll be— I plan to leave a jar of B.J. for Big Baby.

A thank you from a friend.

GLASS, THROUGH A WINDOW

From behind my window pane,
I see a woman of glass
standing on the street corner.

Sodium lights— all purple—
brighten up her chambered spine.
I smell worms and coming rain.

Blacklight curves, her fragile face;
enraptured through the window,

RELEASE THE HORSE

I wish I could close my eyes.

The glass woman does not move,
even as I tap and moan.
She can hear me, I can tell.

I reckon glass is just sand;
she ought not do me that way;
who is she to ignore me?

LITTLE MAN

The little man was dead. Of that, both of the boys were certain. Some time passed before they came to this conclusion, but the assumption was unanimous. For one thing, the little man hadn't moved since they first came upon it in the forest, not even after they crept up beside it and shouted. For another, blackish blood had pooled beneath the little man's body, and thin rivulets eked out across the stone on which it lay.

"What is it?" Alex asked.

"Heck, if I know," Cade replied.

"A little man," Alex said.

The corpse was indeed quite small. Were it to stand, its bald head would barely clear either of the boy's knees. Alex was a year older than Cade, but they were of a similar height. To call the dead thing a "man," however, was up for debate. Unlike their shared stature, the boy's opinions were often each their own.

"A monster," Cade decided.

"The smallest man ever."

"You're crazy."

Its skin was bright and porous like an orange peel and there were more legs and arms than should have been allowed by its maker. The toes and fingers, too, were odd-numbered, had the boys thought to count them. It had a face with lidless eyes and lipless teeth, but no nostrils could be identified.

"How did he die?" Alex asked. The little man had a penis, he'd noticed. The member was loose and clinging to two of the legs. He stared down at it.

There was a wrinkled quality to the thing's flesh that reminded Cade of his Great Ninny laying in her open casket. Besides that, it had no hair and baldness was for old men.

"Done got old," the younger boy determined.

Cade, too had seen the thing's genitalia, but it mattered little to him.

"What about the blood?" Alex pointed.

"What about it?" Cade frowned.

"It's all come out. See?"

Cade pondered this and said, "Got to go somewheres, don't it? I 'spect it comes out of everybody when they're dead."

Alex liked the way Cade talked. There were a lot of things to love about the boy, and his speech-pattern was high on the list. Sometimes, he tried to talk like his friend, but his parents chided the imitations. They told him it wasn't proper to speak that way; said proper language was important for a growing boy. He wasn't sure why it mattered.

"Bet it got bit by a vampire," Alex said. "I will tell you what."

"Vampires ain't real," Cade replied. "A'sides that, they drink of the blood 'til you ain't got no more." He shook his head. "The heck they teach you'ns at that church-school?"

RELEASE THE HORSE

If you forced him to be honest, and he usually wasn't, Cade would admit that he thought little of Alex. The older boy rarely entered his consciousness outside of their quick romps through the woods, if ever at all. He vaguely considered the older boy to be a strange sort; didn't particularly care for the soapy sheen of his hair or the clumsiness with which he carried himself. His folks referred to Alex as that little pervert on the rare occasions he'd had him over to their yard. Cade didn't know what that word meant but knew better than to ask.

"Maybe it fell," Alex said, "like an angel or something." He tilted one hand over his thick glasses and peered up at the heavens.

"Unlikely." Cade pushed air through his teeth. "But I reckon we can find out." He looked about the forest floor until his eyes landed on a sturdy stick. He reached for the branch and hauled it through the grass. "Yessir," he said, and scooched closer to the body.

"What're you doing?" Alex backed away. "Don't touch it," he said.

"Ain't gonna," Cade shot him a look. "That's what the stick is for." He shook it at the older boy.

Alex grew nervous as he watched him wedge the stick beneath the little man's body. He worried it might spring to life, having played dead like a possum. It could lash out at them with those long fingers. There was a name for that, he thought.

Reflexes? He wondered.

"We'll have this figured, tell you what," Cade said. He pushed down on the stick like a lever and grunted. The body was heavier than he expected; the branch cracked in two under the weight. Cade tried it again, and with shorter, studier leverage, the corpse eventually flipped over on its face with a wet smack.

Exposed, the little man bore a six-inch tear down the length of its back. A pinkish loop of intestine had slithered out the gash. Blueish spine-bones glimmered within like a baby's teeth.

Alex heaved. His mouth filled up with drool, and his skin turned the color of ash.

Cade leaned away from him. "Easy, now."

He gagged again, strained against it, and a vein popped open in one eye. Tears of resistance dribbled down Alex's cheek, and blood spread like ink below the surface of the sclera. He swallowed a burp.

"Aw, heck," Cade said. "Don't go gushing on my toes." He drew back his sandals and held out the stick like a shield.

Alex laughed and tried to hold back another belch. Spittle spritzed through his teeth and dazzled like opal dust against the falling sun. "Sorry," he managed.

"Reckon, you might just be right," Cade said. He poked at the innards, and rolled the branch across the flap of flesh along its back.

"So it is a man."

"What?" Cade kept prodding. "Heck no," he said. "Ain't no human bein', I can tell you that."

"Oh."

"But I do believe she may have come out of the sky."

"What do you mean she? Didn't you see? He's got a ding-dang." Alex crouched beside his friend. "Flip him back over, I'll show–"

"Naw," Cade rode and dropped his stick. "Don't

believe I will."

"Okay," Alex retrieved the branch. "Well, I seen it."

"Uh-huh," the younger boy dusted his second-hand jeans. He looked off, deeper into the forest, wanted to be anywhere else. "Gonna have a look around."

"Look for what?"

"Just around," Cade strayed off from the corpse. Away from the other boy. "Havin' a look is all."

"For clues, you mean? To solve the mystery of the littlest man ever?"

"Sure."

Alex flashed Cade his widest grin. "Righty-oh, good buddy."

Once his friend had wandered off into the trees, the older boy's smile faded, and he began to think. His mind fell again to the little man's penis, as it had, off and on, since he first noted its presence. Should he take another look? He was easily spooked, did not typically favor any time spent alone. But some of his favorite activities required solitude, Alex had learned.

He brandished the stick. Sweat formed at the edges of his greasy hair.

Cade had not gotten far before he recalled his missing stick and returned to retrieve it. His sandals padded softly on the moss and decomposing leaves.

Alex hadn't heard his approach.

Cade thought to call out to him but stopped short. From a slight rise, just behind a tree, he watched the older boy work the branch down the shaft of the dead thing's penis.

"Yeah," he heard Alex groan, "stand you up straight like a big man."

The white eyes of the corpse bored into Cade; seemed to beg mercy, pleaded with him to be saved from further indecencies. Blood slithered forth from between the stick and the expanded meatus of its urethra.

Alex held the dead, tent-poled penis between his finger and thumb. "That's better," he said.

A cold sensation gripped Cade by the jaw.

The desire to remain unseen felt like the most important thing in the whole world. He backed away, slowly, and slipped into the folds of the forest.

Cade hurried along for nearly a quarter mile without looking back. He tried to shake the image of what he'd seen Alex doing, but it lingered like the stench of something rotten, a synesthetic bridge in his thoughts which linked the depravity to a forgotten Easter egg he cracked open one July. Cade could smell his own discomfort.

"Gosh-dang pervert," he muttered.

The sky had grown dark, time to head for home when Cade stumbled over a shallow ditch. A twenty-foot rut in the dirt, he discovered, that zig-zagged through the trees. At the far end of the plough-line, he came upon a shattered mass: judging by what remained, it had been a small cylinder before clashing with the upturned soil. It was translucent, purple, and looked much like a tube of glass. The front-facing half had broken open, and a smear of red marked the jagged hole.

Without his stick, Cade prodded at the crystalline wreckage with his sandal sole. For a moment, the substance wobbled, gelatinous, under the pressure of his foot. It hardened, crackled, and a shard punctured the soft rubber and lodged in his heel.

"Hell-fire," the boy shouted.

A furtive movement, something from above, drew Cade's attention away from the pain in his foot. In those expansive nanoseconds, which are only allotted in moments of truthful strangeness,

A bird, Cade thought. But if'n a bird, why the coldness at my back on a warm summer eve?

He turned his head upwards.

A purple tube, intact and gleaming, hovered along the boughs of a birch above; clear as violet cellophane, just like the cylinder at his feet. The tube made a noise, the rumbling of a deep-seated fart, and he watched as it ascended higher.

Fell from the sky, he thought.

Within the airborne chamber, he could see the thing scrabbling around inside. It seemed to shout down at him but he couldn't hear over the dull rumble of the craft. To see one alive and naked, with legs and arms aplenty, Cade decided he had been right too:

A goddang monster.

‡

When Alex had finished with his activity, a sound like thunder cracked the stillness of twilight.

A storm? He worried.

He wondered when Cade would return and remembered the first time they'd met, the second day of vacation bible-school in August of last year. The younger boy had simply walked into the cafeteria and plopped into a seat beside him at lunch. There was a heaping pile of deserts on his paper plate; no proteins or veggies.

"Best get you boys some cake," Cade had said and began to eat. He wore a tank top and bore a remarkable amount of muscle for a kid so close to his age. He hadn't even bothered to introduce himself. "Good shit."

The sparse group of children who chose to sit in Alex's vicinity took to the new boy at once, began to engage him as if he'd always been there. Alex was impressed and had remained so in the ten-odd months since that day. Cade is my best bud, he thought.

SHE CATCHES BIRDS

I's the first to notice the bird last Friday morning. Heard a buzz in one ear while I unloaded my cart and took it for a bumble bee, yellow jacket, some such nuisance. Looked up and seen one of them hummingbirds, just the tiniest of things, so I put down my box of eggplant and went over to the customer service booth.

Too early of a morning for management— imagine that— so I grabbed a radio and called the porter.

"Got us a bird in the building," I said.

"Well, shit," the porter replied over static.

"There protocol for that?" I asked.

I'd never seen a hummingbird come through a store, not in my twenty years working grocery, but did recall reading somewhere that the majority of feathered friends trapped inside buildings die of starvation. I hoped that wasn't true.

"What day is today?" The porter asked.

"Friday."

"Reckon, you got to call the bird people."

I'd been working at this here store for the last six months or so, though not long enough to know anything about bird people. I told Reggie— the porter— exactly that. He sighed and said he'd be right down.

I didn't see him for another half hour, and in that time, I watched the little feller slam itself into the plate glass windows once or twice. The store would be open in another thirty, and I wanted free of my worries before customers started to file in. I felt helpless watching that hummingbird flutter around. Opening shift is bad enough without the extra heartache.

Reggie finally come around the aisle with a broom and dustpan. I hollered for him, and he ambled over.

"Yeah?"

"The bird," I said and pointed to the ceiling. It zipped past my finger and made for the bakery.

"Aw, shit." Cannabis wafted off him in heaving gusts.

I laughed. "Little early for you there, Reg?"

"Huh?"

"You was supposed to give me a phone number. For the—the bird people, you said."

"Right," he said.

Reggie motioned for me to follow, and we headed back to the booth where he pulled a black call-book from the drawer. He thumbed through, pulled a paper card from between the pages, and handed it to me. Bird People was printed across the top of the card in bold; a local phone number, right square in the middle. I picked up the receiver and dialed.

"Heads up," Reggie said and turned back to his broom. "They're weird."

The dial tone chirped in my ear. I flipped the

card over idly: four birds, swallows or finches—something I don't got the name for— were printed in the corners with their wings spread. The middle portion of the card was consumed by a quote or maybe a poem, short- nonsense I couldn't make no sense of:

"From the nest a sun does rise,

And from our heart the kettle cries.

To a feather we often call

That which can eternal fall."

Weird, indeed, I thought, and vaguely hoped no one would answer. The hummingbird zoomed across my eyeline. Seeing the poor thing, I was ashamed, and changed my tune. "C'mon," I said into the receiver.

"Yes?" A voice answered.

"Oh, sorry—I uh—hidy, my name is Jessup and…"

"Yes?" The voice asked again. I couldn't quite place it, age or otherwise. Sorta sounded like a robo-caller. Distant. Too quick.

"Well, we have a bird in the—"

"Address?"

I gave it.

"An agent will be with you shortly. Is that all?"

"It's a hummingbird. Not sure if that makes a difference."

"It does not."

I heard a click. An empty line tone blared into my stunned face. I put the phone down, got back to work, and tried to ignore the little bird.

A few minutes after we opened the store—had a few assholes waiting at the door—a woman walked in and caught my eye right away.

That wasn't so strange, to tell the truth. I tend to notice most females that come through here. Matter fact, I'd already daydreamed an entire relationship with the blue-haired college girl who walked by my produce cart not but thirty seconds prior. Almost like a sickness, you know? One I wish like Hell that I could beat. I been that a'way since I's young. Don't mean to do it. I hate for anyone to feel my eyes and think wrong of it. It's just that them feminine bodies, shapes, angles, curves…It's like they're singing at me.

Prone to get myself fixated, I guess.

Anyhow, that's just to say I didn't necessarily clock this woman on account of all the gear she had on. It was more about the brown hair, thick eyebrows, and unpainted face. That's about all I seen at first.

Then I noticed that the ass was like a steer's. She was soft-bellied, with a tight chest and arms. Her short-sleeved polo, half unbuttoned at the neck, played Hell on my jaw. Had to clamp shut and tuck in my tongue.

Now, like I say, any kind of female is a huckleberry to me— don't got a type, so to speak— but this woman here, she was in a tier all her own.

I did the eyeball dance: looked away, acted like I wasn't giving her the ol' up and down, though that's exactly what I aimed to do. She was wearing some sort of navy fatigues, taught across the waist by way of a thick utility belt. A pair of binoculars bounced against her wide hip and a thick Maglite was ratcheted to her upper thigh, neatly framing the crease of her crotch.

There was a little bird embroidered on her

left breast, like them ones on the card, and the morning's events began to replay in my head.

The Bird People.

When she got past the sliding glass, the woman stopped, put her hands on her sides, and looked up at the ceiling. She turned her head from side to side, long brown locks waving in the door fan, and cinched her gaze. An old man come up behind her—she sorta blocked the entrance, standing right there—and he grunted for her to move.

Boy, she spun around on him so quick, I thought the ol' grump was gonna take one on the cheek.

She muttered something—couldn't tell what—and pointed at her embroidered shirt. The old man stepped around her, straightened his collar all-huffy-like, and made for the display of table-grapes.

When the woman turned back around with a fearsome look on her face, we locked eyes.

My stomach went to feathers, lips waggled themselves into the rough approximation of anxious joy. Her lashes fluttered, she pushed back her hair, and I soared. A returnal smile lit one corner of her mouth before her stare moved to the rafters with blue-steel focus...

Up and away from me.

I returned to earth and tried to go back about my business. Shuttled mangos, broke down boxes, side-stepped customers. Done my best to keep from gawking at the Bird Woman.

Some lady, early sixties, I'd say, come up to me and asked if there was any Japanese yams in back. Normally, I'd have latched onto the old bag with my dreams and eyes. She was six-foot-easy, black dancers' tights, piercing tits; wore a thick bun of tangled grays atop her skull like spiderweb candy-floss... She was really something, and I should have pined for her bony buttocks and thin, amber lips.

Instead, I caught myself scanning the store for blue pants and that head of brown locks.

I lied, told the sexy old woman we didn't get a truck on Fridays, and excused myself.

Pretending like I was going for the toilets, I found the Bird Woman near the water dispenser, spinning a black rope in one hand. I walked past her and seen something silver swirling at the tip of her line.

"Mornin'," she said to me as I scuttled by.

"Hidy," I replied.

She let loose of the rope and it sailed to the ceiling. The silver bit turned out to be a hook, which she deftly yanked against an iron beam some thirty feet above. The Bird Woman pulled her line from where it unspooled within a fanny pack at her hip. A small clasp held an identical hooked rope along her belt line and she quickly wound it around her fist.

"Pretty cool, huh?"

I had forgotten myself; been gawking at her with arms at my sides for God knows how long. My pores puckered with embarrassment. "Sorry," I said. "I'll leave you to it."

"Aw, it's alright," she replied and swung the second line up into the rafters. The hook found its ,mark and the Bird Woman faced me. "I'm used to folks watching."

I took that statement for all it was worth and

stood there while she rigged up a little pulley from a pouch on her thigh. No more than five minutes of cranking line through the well and the Bird Woman had an impressive net strung up between the beams. Looked like someone fixing to play volleyball, some twenty feet off the floor.

To say I's took by the situation would be a vast understatement. Ain't often you find a person living their life with confidence. Most of us go through our days squirming and flailing like bait on a hook, but the Bird Woman had a purpose, and she shined for it.

It was a beautiful thing.

"Now," she said, and yanked on the net, "we just got to find the little guy."

With hands on my hips, I scoured the sky-racks and freezer aisles like I was watching for twisters. "Seen him not too long ago," I said, making a real show of it. "I's the one what called y'all."

The Bird Woman flipped her hair to one side and positively beamed at me. Wet, parted lips. The downward slope of tongue. The wideness of joy. Her teeth were bright and even, and I wanted her

RELEASE THE HORSE

to chew my skin with those brilliant, ivory caps; longed to dive into the warm chasm of her mouth.

I sunk beneath the sun of her gaze and wished happy trails upon my shadows. "Well, I'll swan," she said.

I juddered against the turn of phrase which had not graced my ears since childhood: a common line of my dear, dead Granny.

"Didn't realize I was in the presence of today's hero." She winked. "You're a good'n, ain'cha?"

"That's mighty sweet of you," I said, and couldn't believe I had the courage to say nothing like that to a customer. I'm not the best at sugar-talking and usually never tried. "I's just sorry for the poor feller. Glad they got folks like you to come out and help."

"You'd be surprised how many places let 'em die. Or maybe you wouldn't be." Her smile faded. "People are sick. It's a sad world, I guess."

"Yeah." I looked away, "Well—" I hauled a thumb over my shoulder and made to get on. Figured I best leave her to her business.

"Say, big fella," she cut me short, "wanna give me a hand?"

I said I did, and she offered both sides of the line. I obliged and held onto the net. She unclasped the Maglite from her belt—turned out to be a laser pointer—and I spent the next ten minutes watching The Bird Woman scope the hummingbird through her binoculars.

"Got him," she said.

With the green laser beam, she chased the little thing through rafters, across produce, past the freezers, and eventually, directly into her net.

"Now spin the line!" Her voice was bright, cheery.

I tangled the net until the hummingbird was wound up tight. Looked like a fly caught in a spider's snare. It started squalling up there—the faintest of chirps—and the Bird Woman took the line from me.

Our hands touched. Hers soft and cool. Mine, hot and coated in grit.

Once the ball of net and hummingbird was in her careful grasp, she turned to me. "What time you get out of here?"

In a daze, I told her when, and the Bird Woman

promptly asked me to dinner. We exchanged numbers, walked the aisles together, and parted near the exit. Had to get back to my cart and get through the day with a swarm of wings bubbling in my chest. I said goodbye as a group of customers and co-workers gathered around The Bird Woman to gawk at the rescued hummingbird.

Reggie reappeared and asked what she was gonna do with it. She pushed back her hair and assured him the creature was healthy enough to be set loose.

When the crowd finally let her through the doors, I posted up behind a window and watched her cross the parking lot with the bird bundled close to her breast. I wanted to see her smile when she let the hummingbird free. To witness her joy again, to watch her spin, hair flowing, as the little creature danced away into the wind...

But she didn't.

Still holding it tight, the Bird Woman got into a white jeep and drove away.

Despite the stiffness in my trousers—the idiot grin on my face—I thought less about our date and more about the hummingbird as my shift wore on.

Where did she take it? Had she fibbed to Reggie? Maybe the little feller hurt itself on the windows. She probably just didn't want to whip up a fuss. Kind of like how the grocery store prefers not to call cops on shoplifters. It's a bad look, I guess. I wondered if they had a veterinarian where she worked.

Sure hoped the poor thing would pull through.

‡

First date went well enough that The Bird Woman asked if I'd like to go back to her place. She paid the bar tab—a first for this ol' country boy—and I followed the white jeep in my truck. I put on a Buck Owens tape to gas myself up; The Buckaroos always get me in the right mood. I ain't no celebite, not by any means, but it'd been a spell since my last roll in the hay.

Nerves, I guess.

She lived just outside town in a two-floor cottage surrounded by forest. A nice joint with a picket fence and a greenhouse out back. It was fairly late by the time she led me through the door.

RELEASE THE HORSE

Had me another opening shift on the horizon, and knew I wouldn't catch any sleep if I stayed out much longer. But I figured I'd be calling in sick the next morning.

Didn't wanna rush things, so to speak.

As it turned out, she was the one who got down to business in a hurry. Barely had my ass past her foyer before she had my trousers yanked down to the ankles.

Night sailed past us in a flash as we fucked and sucked our way through the house. I'd never gripped a thigh so sturdy, felt the flip of a tongue that soft, or buried my face inside a furnace of such velvet folds of flesh. She spoke little, screamed herself hoarse, and held onto me like she was fixing to drown.

I grinded my hips and spent myself again and again—fed her open mouth, came upon her rising bosom, against her upturned cheeks—until I thought of nothing at all.

That ain't quite true.

Almost nothing, I should say.

Despite the blissful preoccupation, a

hummingbird flitted to-and-fro in the rafters of my thoughts. As sunlight began to slink beneath drawn shades of the bedroom, I unsheathed my cock from her backside and stretched out on the bed.

"You are a good'n," the Bird Woman said. She lay her head on my stomach, and her lashes fluttered against the rim of my navel. "I'll swan…"

"What'd you do with that hummingbird?" I blurted it out, an accusation which tumbled from my lips before the cum on her thigh had even had a chance to dry.

I felt her eyes open. She was quiet for a spell, then answered, "I let it go."

"Oh," I said.

My body had gone rigid. I knew she felt it.

"It's just that—" I fumbled "—well, I seen you take it with you. Just wondered if it was hurt. That's all."

The Bird Woman sat up, braced herself against the mattress. She let her pendulous breasts sway above me and cast shadows like circling carrion raptors. "You was watching me?"

RELEASE THE HORSE

"Thought I'd see you turn it loose."

"I did."

"Okay."

She stared at me. Searched my face. Deciphered the unanswered questions clotting the edges of my eyes.

"I let it go," she said again and defiance rang out through her words like buckshot.

"I believe you."

"No," she shook her head, "you don't."

I'd seen storms like these before. In my younger, happier days, I'd have weathered it and stayed. As a man with enough notches in the beaten hull of his dick to know better, I rose from the bed and reached for my socks.

Time to go.

"Wait," the Bird Woman said. "I'm sorry. I just—can I trust you?"

Despite my better judgment, I balled up the sock and waited. I looked back at her, saw a mask of anguish replace the brilliance I'd once seen in her face.

Ugliness.

All of a sudden, everything was wrong. I knew I's fixing to hear something I wish't I never had. And then she said it:

"I got worms."

I laughed, and the Bird Woman started to cry. Tears slithered between her lids. My manhood slid up inside my guts.

"The fuck you mean? What worms?"

"You don't understand," she said between sucking sobs. "The worms feel so good. They gave me everything. But there are so many of them. So many inside me, I can't take it. We have to let the birds feed or it's too much. It gets to be too much to even stand or breathe or fuck."

I removed myself from beside her on the bed.

"Don't go. Please, listen! They're so beautiful. They can give you pleasures unlike anything—"

"You crazy bitch."

"Let me show you," she said.

I hauled up my briefs and turned to tell her off again.

RELEASE THE HORSE

The Bird Woman was kneeling on the bed, legs spread wide, arms upturned, outspread, and offered. She closed her eyes and opened her mouth.

I got hard looking at her.

Reckoned I'd pounce, hold her wrists, give her a good, rough goodbye. But then her pores began to swell and pucker; hundreds of thousands of black pits which opened up on every half inch of trembling flesh before me. Whirling voids like hopeful, hungry mouths in the nest of her body.

Had I felt the writhing horde against my cock? Were their sliding, supple movements the cause of my exacerbated pleasures?

I wondered if the worms were catching and wanted to scream. Instead, I opened and closed my mouth in time with her own.

"Here they come," she moaned.

I pushed myself against the blinds, tried to will myself out through the window and away from all this.

"We're gonna—" She pushed air through pursed lips and tipped her head back. The long, dirty waterfall of hair graced the crack of her ass. Her rotund hills—the buoyant mounds over which I'd drooled and licked—were now withered, deflated.

"We're coming," the Bird Woman groaned.

Color breached the craters in her body; bright nubs of greens and orange and blues, like looking down into a carton of crayons. The stubby neon tips began to wiggle and nudge their confines of skin. They rose from The Bird Woman's pores, seemed to sniff and taste the air. All at once, the wriggling multitude stiffened, turned in my direction, their tubular forms lengthening towards me.

"You can't know how good this feels." She panted and sweat gushed from her open pores, drenched the worms in her fluids. "Please, oh please, let us show you—"

As the da-glo parasites uncoiled from the warmth of her insides, her body had shrunken to the size and shape of an average woman. Gone were the indulgent curves and shocking angles.

This returnal state—the normalcy of God's true design—made me as sick as the eyeless multitude reaching out from what remained of her.

I soared through the bedroom—naked and

scared—clenched my eyes shut, flapped myself through that cottage door, and never came back.

‡

Shit flew south after that. Started fucking things up at work. Played hooky for damn near two weeks. I couldn't get out of bed, kept checking myself for holes, and when I finally did show up, I managed to get a complaint filed by a co-worker for lewd and aggressive behavior.

All's I done was ask that cashier for a date. You'd have thought I'd asked the homely sow for a pity-fuck, way she made it sound. Sure, maybe I overextended myself. I know I don't got the best delivery, 'specially when I'm all gassed up. But c'mon.

Look at her, look at me.

You really think I'd stoop so low—?

It's been hard, you know. One minute I's dumping fat loads in the slickest can you ever laid eyes on…And the next, she goes and tells me she got worms. And them worms need culling by way of a goddamned bird.

All I'd ever wanted in a woman and there she

was: Used up, perfect, disgusting.

To say I was in a sore state would be undermining the situation. Started whackin' off all the time. Searched endless piles of free, useless internet porn for someone who looked like The Bird Woman. Bought subscriptions to cam sites after that and found myself looking for tags like #worms or #openpores.

Even got one of them custom silicone dolls from some yay-hoos in Europe. Had it built to the specifications of my fading memories of her. Stabbed holes across every inch in an attempt to mimic her porous nature. But the stern-yet-pillowy flesh I so desperately craved could not be found in the lifeless, worm-free plastic body I had purchased.

All of which drained what little vigor and dollar I had left.

The complaints piled up at work well before the incident. My central manager came by for a visit—she's a fuckin' dime, that one—and said she didn't cotton to the way I's looking at her. Said I was out of line for saying I could see her drawers beneath them yoga pants she was wearing.

RELEASE THE HORSE

Right before they fired me—"Sorry, man. We got a no tolerance policy here"—I swiped the business card from the little black book at the customer service booth. Think Reggie may have seen me do it. Didn't say nothing if'n he did.

Took me a couple days to work up enough nerve to call the Bird People. I sat there, looking at my phone, numbers punched in and ready to go. My hands were sweaty, I could smell the reek of my own breath.

The poem on the back of the card, I flipped it over and read it again—

"From the nest a sun does rise,

And from our heart the kettle cries."

—again, and again—

"To a feather we often call

That which can eternal fall."

I searched for something, some kind of meaning, a clue, please-God-anything; prayed to make this eternal squirming cease to be.

Please, I begged, save me.

Finding nothing, I pressed the call button.

"Hello?"

"Yes?"

"I need to talk to management about one of your employees. Right now. Right fucking now. See, we got a problem here, she—"

"What do you need?"

"She took a goddamned hummingbird, took it home and let it feed off her—"

"Sir, what do you need from us?" The voice was a cold, robotic chasm. No hostility or impatience. No humanity or empathetic tenor. Nothing but a question.

"She's got fuckin' worms goddamnit! Don't you get it? Her perfect, beautiful body, it's all because of them bugs she got in there. She's taking our birds and…God, can you hear me?" There was a pause. I wept into my open hand and let snot dribble down to the floor.

Didn't know what else to say. The voice couldn't hear me, couldn't help. Were they even alive? Was I speaking to no one?

I knew then that I was truly alone and always

would be.

"Do you want the worms?"

I screamed into the receiver.

"Sir? Do you need worms?"

I said I did and gave them my address.

‡

Been working for the Bird People going on a year now. Pay is good. I enjoy the work, keeps me on my feet, so to say. They give me full-time benefits right after the worms took to the ol' husk.

Once the screaming stopped…

That there's a joke, if'n you ain't caught it.

I got two weeks of paid vacation last month. Ain't that something? Went down to see that blues festival they got in Little Rock and met a sweet gal. She likes the worms well enough, gets hot over the hardness of my new body. She don't much care for the way I look when they come out—loathes for them to wrap around her arms, tasting her sweat and tears—but that ain't no care of mine.

We really had ourselves a time.

Hell, I even got me an overtime bonus coming

up at work. That is, if I can make it past the holidays.

See, the thing about having the worms inside you, making you better, stronger, fuller... Shit, nevermind. You can't know what it feels like to have your body open itself up in front of another—to feel with the worms, as the worms—and be embraced as legion, as one.

I guess what I mean to say is, The Bird Woman—Lucinda, that's her name; looked it up in the company directory—she was right. It's all so beautiful.

I keep calling her. Every damn day. I call her over, and over, and over.

Management told me to cool it or else. Threatened to strip me of my bonus. Which I—I mean we—have goddamn earned. They can take this job and shove it up their tail feathers.

I want her back. But she don't answer my calls. Reckon she never will.

BULENDOR COUNTY

It takes a long time getting down to Bulendor County but I would say you ought to take the trip. There is unparalleled beauty in those hills and yonder lies the trailhead which could take us. In regards to natural wonder, I am easily impressed, though that should not deter one from seeking sights of great consequence. We are losing time, and soon, all magnificence will be gone from our world. Maybe this is your last chance to see.

If you care to go, I will follow. What do you say–?

I am pleased with your decision to seize the day and take it by the mane. Bulendor County will renew our faith in stouthearted exploits of all manner. Yes, you will contend with beast, boulder, and bane aplenty. There are the Snapjaw Boys to consider of course; how best to fend off their ornery wiles and salacious predilections. But the 'Boys are rarely active before noon, and I doubt we should worry. What hour do you have by the way?

Goodness gracious, that time already. A late start, I suppose…

Well, we can ruminate on the proper course of action later. For now, perhaps there should be a discussion on how you would like to deal with Stickhands Mason. Far too sharp and much too caustic to overtake by force, I should think. Where is the whistle your Father stole from beneath the Delmar Mounds? It will not be long before his song is required of you. Have you memorized the music to keep Stickhands Mason away–?

I see…

A grave error on your part, that is for certain, but let us pray you will be able to overcome this blunder. God, look down upon this ignorant lamb and forgive the faults of your flock. Amen.

So, tell me about your experience with Bison

RELEASE THE HORSE

Gar. What was the largest bull you brought to ground this year? A three-hundred kilo Gar turned up right here last season; that might be small potatoes compared to what you come across. I know your Mother is a field-stalker of tremendous notoriety and that the horrors scattered across our journey to Bulendor County must be of little consequence to an heir of such esteemed legacy. Also, does your lance collapse or has a powersmith forged you a magnetic compression core? I have not seen you take it out yet, and I wondered—

Oh my. You mean you have never–? This is most unfortunate.

Might I inquire how you first came to this part of the country? I am curious to know what you are doing so close to Bulendor County without the tools your parents bestowed upon your fragile fists. Where could one expect to go without them? You do not know the song and you have not kept a lance or flute. Yet somehow you have made it this far. I do not see how that is possible.

—you say they built a freeway through Bulendor County? And we can just–?

I'll be damned.

THE BAND

Jackson had his dick in his hand when he heard about The Band for the first time. He stood over a hole blasted into the filthy concrete floor of a venue called Publik Haus and watched his piss snake down into the darkness. Jackson was still reeling from the stench billowing up from below when Dale Snakebite sidled up next to him.

Dale's band, Snake Bite Satan, had just finished their set and the shirtless vocalist was still covered in some sort of animal blood. He was as enormous off-stage as he was on, and Jackson felt anxiety needle into his bladder.

Jackson glanced over as the bearded giant wrenched his hand into a pair of tight leather pants. He heard a dull flopping sound beside him followed by several grunts and a tremendous gout of urine.

"I know you," Dale grumbled.

Jackson lurched and his stream withered to dribbles. Ten years in the trenches of extreme music journalism, and he still got pee-shy next to the monsters he wrote about every single night. He kept his eyes focused on the pissing hole.

Snake Bite Satan had been the main event for Jackson tonight and the reason he had waited so long to empty himself. Dale's outfit sounded like your run-of-the-mill Death Metal act on record: guttural growls, gore-bucket lyrics, and saw-blade guitars. All pretty standard, sonically speaking. But Snake Bite Satan had grown notorious over the last few months for an increasingly shocking series of live gigs.

There was the bonfire set outside Juke Blues on the westside, where Dale was rumored to have pulled a burning branch from the flames before swinging it at the crowd and injuring several audience members. Another show had reportedly ended in similar chaos after Dale's lead guitarist jammed a wooden stake into his own chest. Blood poured from the nearly mortal wound in front of fifty shell-shocked heshers in a university basement. One of Jackson's competitors had even written a slam-piece about the band's supposed day-jobs as hardline drug dealers.

This was the sort of shit Jackson traveled four hours to see and it was what his subscribers paid to read about. In fact, his recent article on the rumors swirling around the group had attracted more traffic to his page than he had gotten all year. The response was so overwhelming that Jackson felt he owed it to his readers to make the trip and tonight Snake Bite Satan had made good on that notoriety.

The entire band had emerged one by one from four steel canisters filled to the brim with clotted blood. Dale stomped to the center of the stage, splattering gore with every step and gripped the microphone stand. Jackson was inches from the vocalist as the house-lights went red, and Dale belched a wicked howl from his dripping beard. Hooded stage-hands filed in from the back as he screamed into the microphone. The shrouded figures placed the respective instruments into the hands of the rest of the band and the lead guitarist approached the front of the stage. Jackson noted the satanic strummer's sunken and hollow eyes. A thick-set drummer sat down, and thwacked her sticks together three times. Dale's howl morphed into a shrieking wail and the blood-soaked group whipped themselves into a frenzy which spritzed the crowd in a steady downpour of smelly life-force over the course of their unrelenting twenty minute set.

Jackson's glasses were still flecked with tiny specks of the blood.

"You got that website." Dale continued to urinate with apparent ease. "I seen what you wrote about us."

Jackson's stream suddenly felt in danger of shutting itself off completely; a painful endeavor on any other occasion, and even more so with six cans of Stag sloshing around inside him. He wondered if his line about drug-addled void worshippers was about to cost him his front teeth.

"Good shit, man." Dale squirted a few parting shots and pushed himself back into his pants.

"Thanks-" Jackson said. "Thanks a lot. I dug your—"

"You're wrong though." Dale slapped a meaty palm onto Jackson's shoulder and gripped it tight. Too tight.

Jackson looked directly at Dale Snakebite's eyes for the first time since the hulking mass had left the stage. Under the ticking tube-lights of the Publik Haus bathroom, his face looked older than he expected. The giant's beard was streaked with greys and whites and his long lank hair was thinning out along the back ridges of his enormous skull. The tattoos that dotted his naked torso were faded and bleary beneath all the gore

"Yeah, man. Wrong." Dale let go of Jackson's shoulder and blood rushed back to his nerve-endings. "You say you seen 'em all. The hardest bands. But you ain't seen 'em all."

"Well, yeah, no I mean I haven't seen every—" Jackson felt a little embarrassed as the singer turned away from him. He realized he still had his cock out.

"You ain't seen shit, man." Dale started for the

bathroom door. "You never seen The Band."

"What—" Jackson was confused "—I just saw you guys play!"

Dale Snakebite stood at the exit and Jackson realized how much taller he was than the doorframe. Thick blood dribbled down his hairy back and pooled on the floor. The singer did not turn to face him as he said:

"Not my band. The Band. Something you ain't never gonna see. You ain't allowed," he nearly whispered. "The Band is for us. Things like me."

‡

Jackson spent the next two years with that conversation in the back of his mind. Every band he interviewed, every record he reviewed, and every show he attended, Jackson thought about The Band.

Most of the musicians he spoke with did not understand the question when Jackson asked if they were familiar. Several of them thought he was making Cripple Creek jokes and wondered where Dylan fit into the interview. But a couple of times, his subjects squirmed uneasily or smiled with some vague knowing.

A group of deranged and nameless Mariachi performers from Tijuana, known only as El Cazadors, cackled at him like a pack of murderous hyenas when he mentioned La Banda. And once, a rapid-fire rapper from Tulsa with a predilection for self-mutilation on stage, outright ran away mid-interview; Jackson had casually breached the topic as they shared a blunt stained with the blood of the troubled MC after a particularly masochistic set. There was a glassy fear in his eyes before he turned heel and ran.

Jackson was leery about attempting the question in subsequent interviews, but one night, in the middle of Kansas, he finally heard what he wanted to hear.

‡

It was at a harsh-noise/industrial showcase on the outskirts of the city where Jackson found himself sitting in a barn beside a gas-heater and a performance artist known as Bug. Bug had a set in an hour and graced Jackson with an interview before they took the stage. The two of them sat on hay bales and he steered the conversation from the topic of Bug's new cassette release to the explicit BDSM nature of their live shows. The talk was going well and so Jackson decided to make his move.

"As someone who performs in these dangerous–"

"Thing."

"Thing?"

"I prefer something," Bug laughed. "My identity lies outside of the human experience."

"Oh–" Jackson shook his head in apology "– right, so as something who engages in extreme performance art, do you find yourself seeking out contemporaries? Peers?"

Bug was quiet for a long time. They stared at him with bright purple lenses sparkling beneath plastic lime lashes. Sitting upon the throne of hay, they looked like some aristocratic God of lust and destruction juxtaposed against the harshness of the heartland. Stray bits of hay clung to the static of the metallic green latex bodysuit they wore and Bug put a long claw-tipped finger to full and heavy lips. A gesture of silence.

"I have seen things you cannot imagine," Bug

whispered beside him.

The two of them were completely alone. Bug's hefty crewmen busied themselves with an abundance of Casio synths and sound-boards to be tested and strung from iron chains before their employer took the stage. Bug leaned in closer as if to conspire, as if they were being watched.

"Try me," Jackson smiled, also speaking softly. There was excitement growing in his heart and his groin throbbed absently. "What sort of things have you seen?"

"Bad things," Bug folded a palm over one knee and the sound of creaking latex roared in the quiet. "Things that aren't meant for you."

Jackson felt his journalistic shield slipping from his sweaty brain. He asked the one question he really wanted to know; the only question he cared about anymore.

"Bug, have you–" he watched their eyes " "–do you know about The Band?"

Almost at once, Bug reached out at him. The claws they wore were wrought from copper and they glowed against the gas-flames from the heater.

RELEASE THE HORSE

Jackson felt the warmth of body-temp latex on his flesh and Bug nimbly pulled up the sleeve of his right arm. The latex'd hand was smooth but oddly sticky against him. Jackson had to slow his breathing as Bug's palm ran the length of his naked arm. Searching him, Bug's claws carefully traced the skull and the flying saucer tattooed there.

The copper was sharp and Jackson imagined the hairs of his forearm being sliced away from skin. Bug released him from their plastic grasp and he was immediately cold in its absence.

"Naughty, naughty," Bug waggled a long finger at him. They righted themself back into place on the hay bale. "You have no idea what you speak of."

"So you know what I'm talking about then," Jackson's mouth was dry. "The Band?"

"What you are talking about means nothing to you because you have not seen it," Bug glanced down at the copper claws "Naugh-ty."

"How do you—?"

"The mark," Bug frowned at him and the latex mask they wore contorted in sync. "You do not bear the mark."

"A mark–" Jackson thought of Bug tracing the ink on his skin. "A tattoo? You, what, get a tattoo when you see this band?"

Now Bug was staring at him with something other than the coy amusement of a cat. Bug looked concerned and it made Jackson's skin feel colder.

"The Band," they said. "Not this band, or that band, or band. The Band."

The plastic bodysuit Bug wore had an iridescent quality; not exactly green, but more like the summer beetles that swarmed suburban gardens where he had grown up. As a boy, he had feared them. They buzzed around senselessly, in and out of sight, slamming their tiny beautiful bodies against his own and crawling up his legs. Even then he knew the insects were harmless, and so his fear made him ashamed.

This was the basis for true terror, he often mused: an illogical sense of fright in the face of absolute normalcy.

Jackson was suddenly aware that he felt in danger, sitting here with Bug, and that too smothered him with shame.

RELEASE THE HORSE

"The Band requires a mark," Bug said.

"And you have one." Jackson was near foaming. "Can I see it?"

Bug rose from the hay bale and looked down at him. The gas-fire lit their lavender eyes aflame and they spoke to him once more,

"You can see nothing."

‡

Jackson entered a world of relative success after the interview with Bug. Unbeknownst to him at the time, they had signed a contract with a major label two days prior to the night in the barn. Behind the scenes, the artist had been quietly reinventing themself as a pop-star and the forthcoming record was being hailed as a darkly genius take on populist reconstruction.

By the time Jackson published the article to his website, Bug's entire catalogue had been uploaded to all the big-time streaming services. The physical cassettes reached catatonic prices on the online auction-houses. Jackson himself unloaded his own cassette on ebay for a large sum and felt mildly culpable for the gouging.

Around the same time, the guitarist for Snake Bite Satan had gone missing after posting several cryptic messages online. Jackson covered the strange disappearance and subsequently found himself with several hundred thousand new visitors to his webpage.

The accumulated ad-revenue from the combined successes and losses he covered gave Jackson the most financial relief he had felt in his entire life. A feeling that was hard fought, rarely imagined, and somehow entirely unsatisfying.

The problem, it seemed, lay in Jackson's inability to shake that which drove him to writing about extreme music in the first place: the feeling of fear.

Jackson listened to music, sought out artists, and went to places that made him afraid. The truth of this became apparent only when he felt there was nothing left to scare him. He ached for that feeling. Longed to be shocked into submission and made new as acolyte to whatever audible horrors there existed on the fringe of human expression.

The howls of men like Dale Snakebite no longer kept him awake at night.

RELEASE THE HORSE

The disharmonious walls of horror created by the beautiful Bug did not take Jackson to new realms of terror as they once did.

This loss, he decided, was all in the absence of that which he was never allowed to gaze upon: The Band.

Then one day, Dale called him.

Getting a call from Dale Snakebite was not unusual. Not after the interviews and discussions in the wake of their wayward guitarist's disappearance. What was strange, was that Dale was calling him in the middle of the afternoon. Jackson had learned very little about Dale in their conversations—the singer once hung up on him after Jackson mentioned their conversation that night in the shitter—but he learned that Dale kept the hours of a possum and that hearing from him at eleven a.m. was abnormal.

Without hesitation, the singer told him his bandmate was dead.

"Found him last night," Dale growled. "Sold his guitar and the gear this morning."

"What–" despite having dealt with this nihilistic

abandon before, Jackson was still in awe of Dale Snakebite's removal from human emotion "–what happened?"

"Gutted himself," Dale said. "Again. Got all the way through this time."

"Shit, man" Jackson imagined the guitar player slumped against a grimy bedroom wall with a stake in his chest and death in his eyes. "Have you released a statement?"

"Statement?" Dale sounded drunk. "Snake Bite Satan is the only statement I have to make. We ride on with or without the dead."

Jackson could not decide if what he heard were the words of a salesman most cunning, or the true and honest proclamations of a thing gone mad within the void of hard living and toxic religion. "Well, I could write something–" Jackson began.

"No pussy-shit," Dale cut him short. "I got something for you."

Jackson realized he had not called him for comfort nor publicity in the wake of death.

"The Band," Dale breathed heavily. "They invited him to come and see. I told him they would. Told him to keep on the path and his day would come. The coward couldn't do it. Checked out too soon."

The air around Jackson went electric and he felt the hairs on his body being coaxed from their pores to dance in invisible currents.

"Me and my band, we ain't nothing to this world. No one knows who we are. Aint nobody knows yours neither–" Dale stammered. "But the rules. There are rules. And it don't matter if it's you or him. And he's dead. So it's you."

"I don't understand," Jackson said, though he thought he might.

"I put it in the mail this morning," Dale said and hung up the phone.

Jackson's mind filled up with all manner of bad thoughts, fear, and hot-white anticipation. But mostly he wondered how Dale Snakebite got his address.

‡

Six days passed before it showed up in the mail

bin outside Jackson's apartment.

A box.

Just a normal cardboard box fitting for a pair of sneakers.

An address had been crossed out at the top with a thick black marker and Jackson's own was scrawled hastily below. The return address was listed as a town in Alaska and he questioned if that were true. He opened the box right there on the sidewalk with a swiss-army knife keychain.

Inside the box there was a piece of white computer paper, a green vial the size of a lipstick, and a barbed needle wrapped in cellophane.

Jackson grabbed the paper one-handed and made his way back inside the apartment building. The paper had one block paragraph typed at the top and he read it several times over on the way back to his studio. It read:

THE BAND Requires Your Presence For Your Allegiance To That Which Commands Us. You Are Chosen. Abandon All Aesthetic For Admission. No Jewelry. No Logos. No Text. No Images. No Patterns. No Dark Color.

GENERIC CLOTHING ONLY. Flamboyant Attire DENIED.

Jackson felt his heart sinking. It stunk of art-school buffoonery. Corny, performative...

Hair Must Be Conservative. NO PHONES. No Visible Tattoos. THE MARK Must Be Made Using Equipment Provided. THE MARK Must Be Kept Hidden. This Invitation Is For YOU And YOU ONLY. 1 AM ON FIRST FULL MOON AFTER OBTAINING THIS PACKAGE–

The address listed was residential and only a few miles from Publik Haus. The same place where Jackson last saw the guitarist; the dead man for whom this package was meant for.

He wondered if The Band had come to town just for the recently deceased member of Snake Bite Satan, or if the stars had aligned to make it his lucky night. Junkies don't like to travel.

The former theory made him queasy and he questioned whether The Band knew more about their invitee than Dale had surmised. He checked his phone and saw that tomorrow night was the full moon.

Underneath the address, three final words:

COME AND SEE.

Once inside the apartment, Jackson set the paper aside and pulled out the needle and small glass bottle from the box. He discovered two things: the vial itself was not green but instead held a murky leaf colored ink; when he unwrapped the needle, he found a small slip of paper inside.

On the paper, there was a green symbol and below it The Mark was scratched in emerald ink. The symbol was not what Jackson expected.

After his interview with Bug, Jackson knew a tattoo was somehow part of the equation, and his mind reeled at the possibilities of what it could be. He had spent countless nights trying to recall the markings on Dale Snakebite's naked torso beneath the piss-splattered lighting of the Publik Haus bathroom. He also scoured the internet for images of Bug without their signature bodysuit as he looked for traces of The Mark and nearly convinced himself that seeking a glimpse of Bug's surely-enchanting-flesh did not factor into his nocturnal search histories.

RELEASE THE HORSE

In all of that time, Jackson began to imagine what it was he was looking for.

Some variation on the pentagram? Too simple, surely.

Perhaps a tentacled homage to a Lovecraftian abomination... But even that seemed overly camp for the ambiguous horrors that had sprouted in his mind.

On some level, Jackson worried that this Mark would prove to be a veiled symbol for hate-speech: a rune with racist connotations, or worse, a modified swastika of some sort. Edge-lord attention seeking was prevalent behavior amongst the younger outsiders that occupied his journalistic purview, but Jackson had also learned to anticipate the worst long ago. Sometimes it felt like half his job was spent tip-toeing between landmines of youthful incel-rage and legitimate bigots. It was not uncommon for Jackson to find out a new folk demo he enjoyed was made by a cult of cheese-making homophobes with a history of anti-LGBTQ statements in underground Christofascist circles.

On the paper, The Mark was a small circle, connected to a line, which was connected to another larger circle. Below the big circle was a V shape, followed by another shorter line, connected to an upside down V at the bottom.

To Jackson, it looked like a stick-figure with its arms in the air and a long antenna sticking out of the head.

He carried the little piece of paper over to his bookshelf and studied it intently as he pulled a large book titled Iconography of Hate from the third row. Jackson flipped through its pages for the next half hour, comparing The Mark to various national socialist symbols and skinhead designs.

When he felt secure enough of its general lack of resemblance to anything chauvinist, Jackson moved on to the 'occult' portion of his meager library.

The circles and lines could be interpreted as deconstructed variations on certain Haitian sigils, maybe…And Jackson thought perhaps there was a passing affinity to the hobo hieroglyphs of the Great Depression. But in his mind, the image of the stick-man with a car antenna protruding from its scalp prevailed.

RELEASE THE HORSE

‡

The cab driver was blasting pop-country radio and Jackson's new tattoo was itching like hell. He could not decide which was worse, but the current ditty about "suckin' beer and slayin' deer" was making a strong case. It felt like an eternity had passed since being picked up from the highway motel outside town. Jackson knew they had to be close.

The well-defined fluorescent streets of the minor midwestern metropolis gave way to sinister roads choked with dead winter trees and sloping homes. Ramshackle hovels with garbage mounds that graced their rotting eaves. Here roamed dogs and cats with eyes that flashed strange and opal in the sober sodium street light.

They passed a small child in what was surely the oldest and the filthiest Big Bird costume on the planet. It was freezing out there in the dark, and even at the quick clip the cabbie kept, Jackson could see the wooly cloud of breath pouring from the soiled, tiny beak. As they passed, Jackson's heart heaved at the way the child walked with their pendulous head held down and feathered arms hanging weakly at their sides. Jackson had consumed a heady dose of edible cannabis back in the safety of his motel room—figured a solid head-trip might make the write-up a little more "spicy"—but the Big Bird sighting had already shifted his mood.

"Some people's kids," the cabbie shook his head. "Can't do nothing for 'em. Believe me, I seen 'em all."

"I'll bet," Jackson said. He thought it came out a little more barbed than he had intended. The cab driver didn't seem to notice.

"Hope you stickin' it somewhere warm tonight, Chief," the cabbie said.

Jackson looked out the window.

"Driving out here to the 'Holler, I figure must be some kind of party," the driver smiled at him through the rear-view. "Been to some good parties out here myself," he laughed and sucked his teeth noisily. "Had me some good times."

"What's the 'Holler?'" Jackson asked, unable to stop himself.

The cabbie looked at him through his mirror

and said: "That's hill-people talk for what they call a 'hollow' out East."

Jackson noted that even without the hard 'r' sound, the cabbie could not properly conjure up the word.

"Okay, so what makes this place a 'hollow?'" he asked.

"Easterners call it a town with a valley and rivers, see," the driver went on, "ain't no valleys or rivers round here," the driver flashed him a grin in the mirror.

Several of his teeth were gone, and Jackson figured he knew what kind of parties the cabbie was privy to.

"Us hillbillies call it a 'Holler on account of there ain't nothing on the inside."

It was half-past midnight when Jackson climbed out of the rusty cab and into the frigid wind. The street was quiet, empty, and overwhelmingly dark. At the sight of the empty lots and vacant homes surrounding them, the cab driver had produced a small baggie filled with beige powder. Before he shut the door, he asked Jackson if he wanted to cut out the middleman and get his high.

"Stick with me," he winked at Jackson, "get your high and keep the knife out your belly."

This down-home, junkified bid for kindness almost warmed his freezing heart, and Jackson closed the door to the cab.

There were only three standing buildings within a quarter mile in either direction and so the address was easy to discern. It was a looming heartland manse that had grown heavy with vine and fungus and had been touched by fire or lightning or both. The only sign of life was a gray van in the grass that ticked and dripped from recent use.

The cab wheezed off into the darkness behind him, and Jackson instinctively reached for his phone. He panicked for a moment as he patted himself down but remembered the instructions NO PHONES. Jackson was relieved to recall leaving his cell on the motel bed and began to wonder how early he was. He had considered wearing a watch in the absence of a phone, but the No Jewelry bit seemed dicey.

Jackson followed the dress-code rigorously,

having traded his usual black on black for a plain white crewneck, a pair of faded carpenter's jeans, and his canvas river-shoes. He even took a pair of clippers to his scalp and sheared his signature locks down to the skin. The terrible wind against Jackson's new haircut made his teeth rattle, but the thought of walking into this backwoods trap-house alone was better than the bitter chill gnawing at his skull.

Jackson stood a few yards from the house and took in the area around him. The yard was waist-high with brittle brown weeds and the front porch was packed with so much garbage it looked like the floor had caved in at the middle. The windows were gone and it was pitch as night inside. He pricked up his ears to try and discern the familiar squabble and scratching of a sound-check.

No snare-taps, no drunken chatter, nothing at all.

Jackson was focused on what appeared to be a hole in the jutting roof but could have been a shadow when a light caught his eye. The front door had opened and a wavering torch lit the opening, held by someone unseen. Jackson nearly scoffed at the carnie gag—he had seen too many torch-lit doom metal sets to take them seriously—but caught himself short at the sight of movement on the porch.

In the dim fire light, he could make out several figures standing up among the piles of trash. He wondered how long he had been standing there, staring at these strangers, not knowing they were there at all. Jackson thought maybe they had been watching him the whole time.

One of the figures threw something into the yard and made for the open door. Four or five others rose from heaps of trash to follow, and they disappeared inside. The torch flickered as they passed.

Jackson's legs finally began to move and he waded through dead grasses. He paused to look down below the railing and saw the stranger had discarded a scorched lightbulb. Jackson touched it with his shoe and knelt down to see the melted glass still smoking with acrid powder. He absently pulled up his sleeve and scratched at The Mark tattooed there. When he looked up, a man was knelt down beside him and Jackson yelped.

RELEASE THE HORSE

The man was wearing red cotton shorts and a flannel shirt. He had sandals strapped to his feet and he did not appear to be cold. He was smiling broadly and looking at Jackson with wet teeth. The man watched him rise and stumble away.

Jackson lurched up the squishy wooden step and onto the porch. The man followed him with his eyes and waved. There was something wrong about his face and Jackson turned away from the yard, panic sinking into his lungs. He almost reached again for his absent phone and remembered his keys. Jackson pulled the keychain from his pants pocket. With fingers quaking, he pulled open the miniature blade on his swiss army knife. Jackson held it white-knuckled at his side.

He went through the open door and saw that the torch was not being held from inside, but had simply been rammed into the drywall. It looked like a broom handle and three rolls of toilet paper had been tethered to the top with wire and ignited. It stank of gasoline and Jackson no longer thought of carnies.

"It starts soon," said a voice behind him.

Jackson turned slowly to face the smiling freak

from outside and found him standing nearly toe to toe. He had a wispy mustache and an acne ridden face, but was otherwise a normal looking person. Or would have been if not for the lunacy embedded deep inside his eyes and that haircut. His hair had been clipped with a bowl and Jackson wondered if this psychopath was a metalhead in disguise or an outsider who just looked like that all the time.

What got you an invite to see The Band, Jackson wondered. Just lunacy?

"For Your Allegiance To That Which Commands Us."

Jackson thought of Dale's disregard for human life, of Bug's disconnection from their humanity, and he thought about Snake Bite Satan's dead guitarist; his pale skin and hollow eyes.

Hollow.

"Let me show you," the man said and Jackson could smell a harsh narcotic stink on his breath.

He questioned if the mad man had been the one to chuck the lightbulb pipe in the first place, or if he had only just recently feasted upon its smoking remains.

RELEASE THE HORSE

The man beckoned Jackson with his hands to follow and started down the black hallway. He regretted eating the weed cookies and wondered if you could throw them up and get straight. Jackson took a deep breath, slipped the blade back into his pocket, and followed the man with the bowl cut.

☦

The basement was enormous and seemed to run the entire length of the house above. Jackson had been in similar subterranean show spaces before, but this place had a particular desolation about it.

The area was divided by stone columns, placed seemingly at random, which trickled with slimy green water. Shadows wrestled free from the dark nests in the spaces between these mossy pillars and seemed to lunge out at the dim lighting from a single bulb. In between the rusted pipes and bare-wood slats that covered the space above his head, Jackson could see dangling insulation and ancient newspapers shoved into the crevices. He had been right about the hole in the roof. In fact, the hole burrowed through the floor and went clear through to the basement. Jackson could look up through the hole from underneath and see the cold stars above. It looked as if a God of thunder had chucked a spear of fire through the entire building.

The concrete floor was cracked and littered with overripe garbage bags splitting at the seams.

Ten individuals stood in a semi-circle beneath the naked bulb overhead, and all of them were silent. It appeared to Jackson that he was not alone in cutting off his hair prior to the show: several members of the audience had clearly shaved their heads, and with the loose-fitting outfits, down-cast looks, and low-lighting, they were all remarkably alike.

Jackson wondered how many of them were in bands he had heard of, or even written about. Among them, the mad man with the bowl cut stood rocking himself. The entire group seemed to twitch and bob with something other than anticipation. Even those that were rigid and still had a manner of broiling menace about them. He also suspected the lightbulb pipe had made its way around the whole crowd before he arrived.

His tattoo itched and as he began to scratch at his upper arm, Jackson was struck with another thought: why had no one checked him for The

RELEASE THE HORSE

Mark?

Where was the doorman to pull up his sleeve and check him over for any "Flamboyant Attire?"

Maybe the edibles were making him paranoid.

Perhaps this was all just—

The lightbulb above him popped, and shimmering glass sprinkled down onto his bald head. The shadows burst from their corners, and the basement went black. Jackson let out a fractured wail, and he was alone in doing so. The vast room echoed with his cry and hung there in the abyss for what felt like a lifetime.

In the absence of light, Jackson became hyper-aware of the bodies that lingered in the space around him. The threat of the bowl-cut mad man slithering around in the dark made him gasp for air. He imagined the crowd of plainclothes degenerates reaching for him, their fingers dancing inches from his skin.

There too, was an odor in the blackness. A haunting smell like the gills of a portabella mushroom gone to rot in the cold. It stank of something not quite dead but losing the good fight to a foul weeping infection. There was a tittering movement in front of Jackson, and he put his arms in front of his face to shield himself.

All at once, the light changed in the basement, and he could see what was in front of him.

The full moon had crept through the sky and now hung over the hole in the ceiling. The lunar luminescence filled the void and the underground space was illuminated in wavering shades of silver.

Where the lightbulb had once dangled, there now hung a man with a rope around his neck.

The man was naked, and his feet hovered just over the concrete floor. The rope was tied to a silver eyelet screwed into one of the floor beams above. His neck was so tightly wound that it shot back against his shoulders, and the skin bulged around his tether. The man's protruding tongue was fat and black, and it looked as though his teeth had nearly cleaved the mass in half.

Jackson could tell that he was dead.

He thought he might scream again, but he did not. Instead, he stood there staring at the hanged man, just a few feet away and was silent. His mind shut itself off, and he barely registered the flurry of movement in the room.

Jackson took a breath and watched as four individuals removed themselves from the circle of ten.

One of the four rammed her boot into a bag of trash and bent down to stick her arm into the hole. The tallest of the lot stood in front of Jackson and reached up into the insulation with his bare hands. Two others, including the bowl-cut man in the red shorts, rummaged through an enormous pile of garbage behind the hanging corpse.

The remaining six all watched quietly at what was happening around them.

From one bag of trash, a two-by-four wrapped in wires and cords was produced. The tall stranger pulled another similar-looking contraption from inside the ceiling, and Jackson stood frozen. The bowl-cut man and his companion pulled a series of cast-iron pots from their heap of garbage and scattered them at the dead man's feet.

As the tallest moved past Jackson, he got a good look at the wooden plank he carried. It was a makeshift instrument with rusted strings and some sort of electric wiring soldered to the surface. He did not look at Jackson as he strode into the darkness and he immediately reappeared with two particle-board boxes under one long arm. Mismatched extension cords hung from the boxes, and both had similar voltaic switches with sheets of gauze nailed over the front. Jackson could see the gauze sheeting was stained and punched through with several dozen holes. The tall one set the crates down heavily on opposite ends of the hanging body, and he pulled both cords over to an electrical outlet.

The rustling and clanging made by the four as they set up around the corpse were the only sounds in the basement. Within moments, the four had assembled in a separate semi-circle within the remaining audience. The tall one and the booted stranger stood to either side of the corpse with their plywood guitars. Each plugged their respective boards into the gauze-covered crates and flipped switches that snapped loudly in the quiet. Bowl-cut had organized nine black pots in front of him and he knelt on the floor. His companion stood across from him beside a large iron cauldron tipped on its side with a wooden stick in both hands.

Without warning, the tall stranger pulled at a rusty string on his instrument, and the basement filled with sound.

The noise hung there in the air around them, and for the first time, the six bystanders moved.

A couple of them put their hands over their ears, and a woman on Jackson's left banged her bald head. She stomped her foot so hard in triumph Jackson could feel it in his shins. He heard someone else vomit beneath the wave of noise contained in that one single note. Another hollered out with joy.

Jackson wept.

The sound slowly faded, and the woman in boots picked up a string between her fingernails. Jackson watched her viciously yank the cord to one side and let it go with a smack. The note it produced shot out into the audience and Jackson cried so hard his stomach ached.

The percussionist smashed his stick against the upturned cauldron, and a thunderous roar blasted across the concrete walls. It reverberated in and out of the darkness. Back and forth.

On the floor, the bowl-cut man rattled and tapped his iron pots. His eyes were closed, and his mouth was open. The cacophonous beat pulsed through the air and made Jackson's skin itch. The sensation was maddening, and he realized he was scratching his arm. He absently considered the wetness on his fingers. The rat-tat-tapping circled his brain, and the booming made his gut bounce, and now his entire body itched.

The bowl-cut man held up his sticks, and they looked like old-fashioned bunny ears, a television receptor snapped in half like a wishbone.

Jackson thought of The Mark…He looked up at the rope, and it dawned on him.

The corpse moved. A dead man's tongue waggling between teeth. Open eyes. The body did not struggle or claw at the rope about his neck. His greenish arms spread wide from his sides, and he lifted them high over his head. His hands opened, fingers splayed, and the guitarists below picked their strings.

The notes wrapped around each other in a sound akin to a Japanese biwa on fire or a cello plucked by wriggling centipedes.

RELEASE THE HORSE

The corpse spread his legs at the disharmonious sound and the percussionists took to beating their iron. The Band played as one, and Jackson knew that The Mark on his arm was the hanged man. As he watched and listened, Jackson put his hand in his pocket and pulled out his keychain. The tiny blade was still open, and it was a miracle it had not cut his thigh to ribbons. Jackson looked down at the knife and walked up to the dead man. The music sizzled and snapped in his ears. He craned his neck to see the corpse's face, and he approached a moldy amplifier.

Jackson stepped up onto the box, and the tall guitarist paid him no mind. Jackson was just high enough that he could reach, and he began to saw the rope around the corpse's neck. Jackson was not sure how long it took him or if The Band watched him do it, but eventually, he got through the cord.

The body fell heavily to the ground. He watched it fall and thought it looked so bizarre with its arms stretched open. The fall was not long, but the dead man's head cracked against the concrete. Blood pumped out from each side while The Band continued to play.

Jackson got down from the amp.

He walked back to his place in the circle, and the dead body twitched. Blood spurted onto his ankle as he passed, and it squelched under his sneakers. A shadow rose behind his back and when he turned around to see, the corpse was standing.

The Band beat their instruments furiously, but their bodies barely seemed to move.

The cadaver opened its mouth and began to sing.

Eyes open, filled with white.

‡

Jackson woke up on the basement floor. The woman who had stood beside him was gone, but there was a dried puddle of vomit, and someone else was hunkered in a corner, shitting noisily.

He stood.

There was a pool of blood in the center of the room, and morning sunlight beamed down on the puddle. A long rusty streak led away from the thick, sticky mess and stopped at the base of the stairs. Jackson went up the staircase and back down the decrepit hallway. He passed the hole by the door, but the torch was gone.

RELEASE THE HORSE

Jackson walked away from the house and passed the lightbulb pipe. The grey van had pulled out from the yard and left two muddy trenches in the grass. There was even more trash in the street than he had seen under the veil of night. Needles and diapers, hundreds of silver baggies once filled with gas-station spice.

He was amazed to see the familiar cab parked across the street and even more so as the cabbie came waltzing out of a nearby hovel.

"Hey," Jackson said, hoping for a ride. He crossed the road quickly.

The cab driver turned around, and he looked hung-over. He smiled at Jackson and wiped at his eyes. The cabbie appeared a kinder, gentler soul in the morning rays and he was thrilled to see a friendly face. A normal face.

"Mornin, chief" he said.

Jackson pulled the little knife out of his pocket. He punched the blade into the cabbie's temple and pulled it back out. He did it again, and blood whizzed out around the blade and through the hole. Jackson's fist was covered in gore, and he pulled it out and slammed it back in. The cabbie's face went slack, but he was not watching him.

Jackson stared at the little hole he was making and wondered if there was anything else inside.

Was it hollow?

The driver slumped back against his car and slid out of Jackson's reach, taking the swiss-army knife with him. Jackson looked down at his hand, and he heard an engine approaching.

From the corner of his eye, he watched the gray van back up behind the blood-soaked cab. Jackson saw the back door open, and the tall player climbed out. The passenger door swung out, and the pumpkin-pie haircut psycho walked up to him with a rope in his hands.

The tall one did not look at Jackson. He grabbed the cabbie's left leg with his long arms and dragged him over to the van. The bowl-cut man knelt down and put the rope around the cab driver's neck. The meth-mouthed driver made gurgling noises and sounded like he might drown.

Bowl-cut looked back over his shoulder at Jackson and smiled. Then, he turned back to his

RELEASE THE HORSE

work and looped the rope into a knot. The tall one grabbed the other end, and all at once, both members of The Band pulled. They jerked the rope so hard Jackson heard the bones snap inside the cabbie's throat.

The gurgling stopped.

The bowl-cut man let go of his end and got back inside the van. The tall one heaved at the rope, and the cabbie flopped over like a fish. His bleeding body was dragged head-first up into the back of the van. An arm shot out of the driver's side window and gave Jackson a wave. The tall man shut the door, and the van pulled away slowly. Jackson watched it turn a corner, gone from sight.

THE FAMILY WHISTLE

"Sit here," Uncle said, "and listen."

"I don't want to." The boy shook his head.

"What did you say?" His voice rang out like a shot.

"Mind your Uncle," Papa called to the porch from the kitchen. "Don't make me come out there."

"See," Uncle said, "got yourself in trouble."

The boy stood. Tears welled in his eyes.

"Your kid ain't listening, Earl."

A clattering of dishes; Papa's footsteps.

"Uh-oh." Uncle smiled. The trenches of his teeth were grey. "You're in for it now…"

RELEASE THE HORSE

"Okay," the boy said, voice rising. "I'll listen!"

Papa's footfalls stopped short of the screen door.

"That's better," Uncle said. He reached inside his checkered suit.

The boy sat. He heard Papa retreat to the sink.

Uncle produced a wooden reed no wider than a blade of grass. He put the stick to his lips and blew; a sickly scream whistled out, impossibly loud. The boy winced.

Inside the house, Papa began to howl. Porcelain shattered against a wall. Papa's legs kicked at the floor, a full sprint for the porch. The boy began to cry.

"Now, now, nephew," Uncle stood and hopped off the deck. "No crying." He backed away.

"It won't hurt much," Uncle said with both eyes on the door.

INCIDENT AT THE TANEY POTLUCK

Don't reckon I could say how I got here. Not in a way that'd make a lick of sense to the likes of y'all. Ain't in the best shape for tellin' no tales anyhow. Figure you already seen my wounds. Guess you might think you know what's been goin' on out'chere in these woods.

That right, Mister?

Understand the sitch'ee'ation, do ye?

Was me what done it? Killed them folks—slipped the guts out their bellies–?

RELEASE THE HORSE

Do I got it straight, buddy boy?

Well, let me tell you a thing or two. I'll give y'all what I know about them woolybuggers down on Taney bluff…

I'd been workin' guard at the fancy museum they put up down in Arkansas. That one out past the college town. Real high-class joint, that museum. Art from all over the world. Famous shit– stuff I seen in textbooks, like when I's in elementary school.

Wife of the Dollar-Mart people was the one what staked it. Some ol' bitch with too much money and not enough time on her hands.

Whatever sins those Dollar-Mart motherfuckers had hid up their cunts, they sure as hell tried to pay it down with all them paintings.

Most of my coworkers was goin' to school at the art college, next town over. Them kids all worked of a night so's they could net a few hours after class, which is how I landed the mornin' shifts.

Never went to no university myself. Grades, absences, diss'plinary action… I'm good on all that. More of what you'd call a self-made genius, I guess.

Just a hair older than them kids, too, if that ain't already obvious.

Anyhow, it were an easy gig. Nothin' to fuss over. I liked the early hours, got paid a decent wage, and not much to do 'cept mill around makin' sure tourists don't get too close to the 'Vinchis and Goyas. Ladies didn't particularly care for the No Backpack policy, but it weren't hard to enforce.

Ma'am! Keep them straps off your back! Sidesaddle only, if'n you please. You know, that kinda thing.

A real breeze compared to the year and a quarter I spent chuckin' drunks out the door at The Tick. Bar jobs ain't worth the hassle, you ask me. 'Sides, a man with my intellect needs a sight more stimulation than moppin' up barf off the floor.

Surrounded by the great works of man, I was a happy camper. Inspirational shit, you know?

They was one specific painting that always caught my eye: an untitled piece by this feller called 'Ronny-Maus-Bosch. Whopper of an oil paintin'. Stretched from one wall to the other in three separate panels. Oak, I believe it was.

RELEASE THE HORSE

First time I ever laid eyes on Eugene Daughtry was right there in that room beneath the Bosch painting. Bet'ch'all know that part. Guess Mister Belvin told y'all 'bout that day.

You talk to him? My supervisor? He can tell it better'n me.

Fine. Sure. I can give ye my account. Whatever you say, Chief.

So, I's on the tail-end of my shift—you know how that is—and just about whipped from shepherdin' a tour-bus of Norwegians all goddamn day. I's so beat, in fact, I figured I'd spend the last half hour in my favorite wing of the museum.

They got this whole section filled with craziest shit you ever seen: religious stuff, Jesus', mostly, and a fair amount of real estate devoted to Hell. Or what we Christians call Hell, anyhow. But it weren't your typical fare…Bloody whips, rotting corpses of Christ, demons with faces where buttholes ought be.

Real wild stuff.

Even had this box—gold and crystal—with the dried-out vocal cords off one of them Greg'rian monks inside of it. You know, the ones what did them chants. Poor dead bastard was 'sposed to have sung like a genu'wine angel of God. Looked like beef jerky to me.

They had the ol' 'Ronny Bosch painting hung right beside that case, which is where I liked to stand. Felt special in there. Intense, like.

You could look up at that thing—the Bosch— and always find somethin' new: an egg with lizard's legs walkin' backwards, or a little girl with fingers for hair; holes the size of four-wheelers along the side of a cyclops' jaw.

I's downright hypnotiz'ized by it.

Sometimes got the feelin' them little buggers and goliaths would shimmy across the canvas when I weren't looking. Whirling carousels of ghouls and m'amphibians. A kaleidoscop'tic nightmare in paint.

I's zonin' out, watching the painting, when Mister Belvin walked in.

Far as bosses go, Mister Belvin was a purty good'n. He didn't take no shit, mind you. Real stuffy type. But s'long as you did your job, he

RELEASE THE HORSE

weren't gonna bring you no static.

On account of that, I straightened up right quick when I seen him come strollin' in. Put my head forward, arms behind my back, a quick nod.

Belvin was wearin' a navy suit, starch-sharp as always, but he had this funny look on his face. Worried.

'Fore I could even say hidy to the boss, 'nother man walked up behind him. He was a real big feller, gray whiskers, bone-white suit. Looked old-timey. Had this wide-ass Stetson on his head. Barely made it through the door with that thing.

Big money type.

I's so fix'tated on the look of him that it took a few passes til I seen the lit stogie 'tween his fat fingers. A big, brown log slobbered in drool. The stink of burnin' shit and wet cinder.

The fuck–?

Reckon my instinct'chool habits done took over, and I come dashin' right up to Mr. Blevins and this cigar-puffin' heretic. Just who did he think he was, sullyin' such great works of art with his dingy stubber smoke? I mean, Christ-in-heels, the damn

Bosch was right there!

Can't have a gift to humanity smellin' like Meemaw's trailer, now can we?

Held my hand out like some kinda traffic-pig and opened my big, dumb mouth to holler: Halt! You there! You with the smoke! Put that dag'nabbin' cigar to your boot and drop it in your suit-pant before I—

But then Blevins put his hand out to stop me. The boss turned his eyes so sharp theys set to filet my ass from temple to trousers. He pursed up his lips and give me a look that said: Don't you dare come no closer. Not another step, you dadgum fool! Don't you know who this man is?

I stopped short where I stood, tongue droopin' from my mouth. What the hell you mean? I asked Blevins with the bulgin' of my eyes. He's smokin'! I cried out by the crossin' of my arms.

Mr. Blevins sneered, and his face turned to beets. He waggled his ringed fingers at me: Fuck. OFF!

"There a problem, Percival?" The stranger asked from beneath his hat. Fresh smoke coiled through his mustache, and he snorted up the stream through ruddy nostrils.

"Why, of course not, Mister G," The boss-man said. His voice rose high and girlish. "Let us head to the Egyptian Wing, and I'll show you the–"

"Seems to me like your man here had something to say," Mister G said, ignoring Blevins. He locked eyes with me, a funny lil possum's smile at the corner of his mouth.

"Never mind him, he was just leaving." Blevins smoothed his fancy-pants suit jacket. "Weren't you?"

"Yessir," I said and practically jogged myself the hell out of there. "Pardon me, gents."

"Hold it right there," Mister G's voice rang like chimes on the wind through the gallery. "What's your name, son?"

I stopped and turned back.

Mister G took off the Stetson and held it like a grievin' pastor before his flock.

Mr. Blevins looked back and forth from me to he, wearing a face I ain't know how to describe.

Fear for things beyond his control, maybe.

Well, anyhow, I give the man my name, and we shook hands. His palms were chill and rough as a Chore Boy. Reeked of tar soap and ashes. He give me a funny feelin' somewheres deep down, like the time I's over to Booger Mayhew's place and he brung out the ol' coyote he kept for a time. Pettin' that coyote brought on the heebie-jeebies somethin' fierce. Didn't seem right. Like I weren't supposed to have laid hands on such a thing, you know?

Y'all must've felt that a'way when you picked up The Backpaddle Strangler few years back. Bet that feller was a real trip. You the one what brought him in?

Thought so.

So, like I say: was the end of my shift, and even though my run-in with Mister G left me shook, the WWE was on in an hour, and I's needin' to get home. But not two beats after I shoved my shit into the locker and grabbed my keys, the boss-man come up behind me.

"Well, well, well," Mr. Blevins said. "Someone

has made quite the impression on our esteemed patron."

Nearly shit my britches, tell you what.

"I'm awful sorry, sir," I said. "Sure didn't mean to—"

"Please remember," Blevins cut me off, "if you see a member of management with a guest, do not interrupt. You have no idea what that man means to this establishment. No clue as to what he has given us."

My heart sank to my busted knees. Reckoned it was time to clear out the locker I just got through packin'. Here come a month or more of applications and pointless interviews. Newspaper ads and wanted-signs in windows. The hopelessness of it already ringin' in my red ears.

"However," the boss-man held up a finger, "Mister G was most impressed with the way you conducted yourself this evening. So enthused by your attentiveness, in fact, that he has decided to offer you a job."

I stared, mouth open.

"Nothing permanent, mind you, but for a

weekend's work, you will be paid handsomely. More than you have ever earned, I should imagine."

He told me how much and that a shuttle was to fetch me come mornin'. Said to pack light but to bring fresh uniforms. Then Blevins give me a nod and walked right out the door.

That was it.

Cain't say I's too fond over the boss assumin' A.) That I'd take the gig, no question– and on a holiday, mind you–and B.) The general state of my finances prior to takin' up the glorious mantle of protectin' his grand halls of paintings and sculpture.

I didn't let on to my bein' pissed on account of him bein' right on all counts.

So, the next mornin', I pull up to work on my bike, and sure enough, they's a damn bus waitin' in the lot. And I could tell right away it weren't to bring in no tourists.

For one, it was too early of a day. Least another hour 'fore we'd see any folks waitin' in the lot. But I also don't recall layin' eyes on nothin' quit like it: used to be a stub-nosed school bus, I can tell ye that much. Short little deal, like the ones you see shippin' kids out to the farm schools. Purty small classrooms ou'chere.

Anyhow, it weren't a school bus no more. Somebosy had decked that puppy the-fuck-out with all manner of polished chrome and a pearly white paint job.

I tell you, that was one hell of a fine shuttle bus.

Driver took my bag. A real nice feller called Ray—y'all talked, I'll bet—and he told me to take a seat.

I climbed my happy-ass aboard and ain't no braggart when I tell y'all I felt like a goddamned king. Velvet seats. Stocked bar-cart. Pack of Benson & Hedges on a marble tray. Clean as a whistle.

Ray said it'd be a couple hours drivin' as we pulled out the parkin' lot. Asked if they was anything in particular, I'd like heard on the stereo to pass the time.

"Play me some Possum," I declared, and cracked the seal on a bottle of rye. I could tell Ray knew the drill by the cut of his jaw and were pleased to hear the voice of ol' George Jones singin' the gospel of my youth. I pulled a smoke from the pack and cranked the window.

"Ray, my man," I said and torched the ciggie, "I do believe I could take a ride like this'n for all my remainin' days."

And that there was a fact, Jack. Smoothest wheels I ever rode. Most plush'n'est seats I ever sat. What a trip.

I ain't so good with directions—one o' my sore spots, I guess—but eventually, I realized we weren't in Arkansas no more. Vine choked concrete and deep, heavy woods give way to tricklin' creeks and open pasture. The two-lane'r we was on ramped up to a six-wide freeway lined with hay bales. Less folks of a wanderin' type, more big-rigs, and wild-eyed hitchers.

"We in Missouri?" I hollered up at Ray.

"The one and only." He beamed through the silver-wrapped mirror.

"Why they call it the Show-Me-State?" I asked. Not sure why. Never could make no sense of it, and just wondered if he knew, I guess.

"Wasn't always called that," Ray told me, "The

Cave State, used to be."

"That so?"

"More lies beneath these hills than any man could ever possibly know. Slow, rolling waves of green which once comprised the oldest American mountains; cavernous wonderlands, endless worlds below. Secrets of the earth. Boundless mysteries."

"Uh-huh," I nodded. Smoke was makin' the headlight, and Ray's conversation weren't assuagin' my ails. George Jones sang about something real sad and I fidgeted in my seat. "So how come they changed it? Show-Me-What, am I right?"

"I'm not too sure on that one." Ray chuckled. "But I do know this: if you lift the right stone in our part of the world, there is so much to see."

Lookin' back on how things was soon to traspir'ate, I cain't help but to wonder if Ray knew what was what. Seemed like a sweet guy, you know? Lil off-the-trail, so to speak, but didn't strike me as the sort would play cronie to a bastard like Mister G.

Takes all kinds, I guess.

Well, we carved our way through them Ozark

mountains til Branson come into view. Ain't been down this way since I's just a child. Never cared for it. All them flashin' lights and two-bit Yoakums. Crawlin' with tourists. All fuss and no culture.

Guess I better get used to it, huh, boys? Figure maybe I'm here to stay. Reckon I'll be somewheres off the strip, though. Least there won't be no tourists.

Shoot, y'all got me tore up.

Where was I?

Once we got clear of the main drag, Ray pulled the bus up through what looked to be a service road. Just a gravel trail, really. Barely room to piss with your legs spread. Forest through there was dark and old. Quiet too, I'd wager, if Possum weren't cranked to ten on the stereo.

After a half hour of climbing stone, the bus come over a rise. Woods was still thick as could be, but some fool had gone and dumped a mansion right in the middle of it. It were a massive sucker. Brick and oak. Three standin' rooftops with spires to heaven. Sprawlin', you might could say.

Once we got up to the house, I could feel a

breeze whippin' at me and knew we was above water.

Sure enough, Ray told me: "Mister G and his guests will be arriving at the dock any moment. Please drop your bag off in your room—eleventh door on your left—and meet me back here on the porch."

I walked into the front room, and the house was about what I expected. Won't go into all that. Know y'all been up in there. You seen the taxi-dermi-ficated elephants, bears, and big cats and shit. You know what kind of place it were. Old world stuff. Brass and crystal doodads ever' which place. Furniture what looked to have been older'n the riverbeds.

Dollar signs, buddy.

Nothin' but money-money-money-money.

My room was about two mile down the hall, I found out. You hear "the eleventh door," and figure it must be like a hotel type sitchee'ation, then you get to walkin' and you start askin' how big a home could actually be. And if'n it's so big, is it really even a home?

Anyhow, I left the bag on a quilted king-size and got back out to the yard like Ray said to do. It'd got hot out with the five o'clock big'un beatin' down on me. Started gettin' nervous about what exactly they was gonna have me do. I hoped Blevins hadn't told no fibs about what kind o' guardin' I did for the museum. Hoped it was gonna be a laid-back gig.

Ray must've smell't the fear sweatin' off me cus he turned to give me a lil smile. "Tonight will be a lovely affair. You'll do just fine." He winked.

That made me feel better—some, at least. Breeze picked up and cooled my heels, too. Was just about to ask Ray if I had time to light one up when I seen a trail of dust come up the hill.

A big, black 4x4 hitchin' a cherry pontoon roared over the rise and bumbled down the drive. In the front seat, I recognized the massive Stetson—couldn't figure how he kept it on inside the cab—and a bright red stogie coal at the wheel.

Ray held up one hand at the truck, and I fumbled mine from the back of my britches to parrot.

RELEASE THE HORSE

All six doors seemed to snap open at once and several pairs of legs dropped to the yard. Everybody moved so quick it were hard to make eyes at any one in particular. A frenzy of fur shawls and bustlin' dresses. Pinstripe suits and crazy gesticulatin'. Gusts of cognac, impatient perfumes, and a righteous human funk. The group ranged from small to tall, but each and ever' one seemed to tower over me.

They twirled past like a twister in May and didn't pass me so much as a sideways glance.

"Right this way," Ray said behind me, and I realized he'd slipped back to open the door for the guests. I stood there like a fool tryin' to make sense of who and what I's in the presence of when Mister G grabbed my shoulder.

"Hidy, big feller," he said. "Welcome."

I stammered out some awkward greetin', and he just stared at me. Had that lil smile buried in his whiskers. Felt like a steer at the county fair come late Sunday.

"The kitchen is prepared for you, sir." Ray said at the door. "All staff have vacated the premises."

"Very good," Mister G said, still watchin' me with them proud, father's eyes.

"How was your excursion to the docks this morning?" Ray chimed.

"Fine, fine," Mister G answered. Finally, his disconcert-alatin' gaze drifted off from me. "Poor Miss Detta got sick on the boat. Bless her heart. But the lake air does a body good. She'll be alright."

I made to turn back to the house but Mister G grabbed me again.

Was gettin' a lil tired o' that, I can tell you. Don't like for nobody to put hands on me, let alone my current employer. Struck me as unprofessional.

"Did Ray here show you the back deck? Overlooks the dam. You can see damn-near all of Taney Country from this bluff. Been in my family for—well, a long time. It's a special place. Subterranean falls are currently dumping six and a half thousand cubic feet of water per second beneath our bodies at this very moment. Untold mystery in the canyons and chasms below. Fantastic sights and sounds, forever unseen."

I said that Ray told me much of the same but

didn't wanna let on as to how uncomfortable that talk was makin' me. Reckon he could smell it on me anyhow. Just seemed like the type to know when another man's plums have shrunk with fear.

Mister G rolled his stogie 'cross the lips to be brushed by his whiskers and asked: "Do you know why you're here?"

I told him I expected to be doin' some guardin' on account of Mr. Blevins' request to pack a uniform.

"I like your cut," he said and nodded. "You were fixing to throw me out for smoking at the museum."

"I didn't know who you was at the time, or else I'd never—"

"Hogwash," Mister G waved me off. "You've got a strong will to protect and serve. I could see it in your eyes. You'd have crammed my cigar in the trash if your boss hadn't told you to keep those mitts off the money-tree."

Weren't much I could say to that.

"Let me ask you this instead." Mister G took off his Stetson and wiped at his spotted brow. "Do you know who I am?"

"No sir," I admitted. "Just that you done a lot for the museum. I figured maybe you was part of the Dollar-Mart family."

Mister G laughed in my face.

Guess I was wrong. Ain't give it much thought up to that point. First thing what come to mind when he asked is all.

"What if I said the Dollar-Mart family has a boss," Mister G said. "And that boss has a boss… And on and on and on up the line, there's lil' ol' me."

"So, what, you're like the Guv'ner–?"

"That ass-for-a-head lingers somewhere around tier-three, if you catch my meaning."

I didn't, but made like I did with a nod.

"Everyone you'll meet tonight is of great value to the Ozarkian State. To be here, among us, is not something many folks come to witness. We are a…unique group of individuals, who, through our various wealths and industries, advise and administer pivotal designs to the greater Ozarks, and—"

RELEASE THE HORSE

He went on like'at for quite a time. Never thought he'd shut it down. I didn't take too much away from all of his hoopla, to be honest. Hard to follow what he was sayin'.

Muddy-talk, my Meemaw used to call it. Stirring up what's clear with nonsense words.

Even if he weren't talkin' plain, I could tell he wanted me to know how big a boy he was. Made double clear by the paperwork he had me sign once we come inside. Said it was binding–A Big Deal–and that I weren't to say nothing to nobody; that if I was to disobey the NBA, it'd be trouble.

What the NBA, of all things had to do with it, I don't know. But he said unzippin' my lip meant hell all the way down.

Fuck it. I signed it. O'course I did. Kind o' money they was givin' me? Shoot.

You'd have done the same.

After I signed them NBA papers, Mister G had Ray take me into the dinin' hall. My God, that were one mighty table. Did y'all know they made 'em that big? Sixty-nine seats, all told.

Counted ever' chair my damn self.

Paintings all over the walls in that dinin' room, too. Fancy shit I ain't ever seen nor even heard of. Expensive stuff, for sure, but nothing like what they kept at the museum. I seen one with a black face covered in moss or some kinda infection. 'Nother had a nekkid woman with arrows stickin' out the body ever' which place. Monsters. 'Bominations. Crimes against God.

Nasty work.

I did recognize one familiar piece up on the wall. It were a big, long, three-panel deal. Oak, for sure. Along the grey-green fields, critters of all manner strutted their stuff in bizarre parades of horseplay. Puckered holes and bug-eyed wonders. Cork-tailed lizards. Candle-wax ears.

That's right: they had a genu'wine Ronny-Maus-Bosch, right there above the head of the table.

Sort of threw me, you know?

Of all the things I thought rich folks was capable of, owning a thing like that weren't one of 'em. It just didn't sit right. Ain't a 'Ronny Bosch painting s'posed to be in a museum? Don't we all deserve to see the lil scamps and bingbongs he come up with way back when? That there's history, dammit!

Never give money too much thought 'fore I come here. But I tell you what, that shit stuck with me. Nowadays, I think about it all the time.

Money, I mean.

Who am I kiddin'. Y'all don't care 'bout none o' this. Why would ye? You just want the blood'n'guts. That's what they pay y'all for. Well, it's a'comin', goddammit. You'll get it.

It's comin' alright.

Right 'fore he left to fetch the folks for dinner, Mister G told me what was what.

"You're probably wondering why I brought you here," he said. "Once a year, I host a gathering of our region's finest patriots. The real movers and shakers. If the Ozarkian State is America's forgotten kingdom, we are its forsaken Lords and Ladies. Shepherds of hard times to come. For in a world driven to cinder and blaze, these Ozark waters shall remain. To a future Hell where the sun has no master and seas reclaim the shore, our cavernous domain will serve as a fortress to those who can claim this land as blood. We suffer no pilgrims, will take not the unsheltered. Outsiders be damned! For what have they given us if not a lifetime of scorn? Shit on the coast, we say. Hold no quarter to any city-rat foreigner who would not have pissed in our land lest their own was stripped and taken by the fires of 'civilized' progress."

He give me a look like I ought have somethin' to say. Just sort o' stood there. Nodded.

"But tonight–" Mister G donned his Stetson "–we celebrate."

"Well, uh," I stammered. "Congratulations on all that. Or sorry, I guess."

The old man laughed. High and mean. "How true," Mister G said. "How true indeed. Tonight, we will feast on handcrafted plates of our region's finest delicacies. Rarefied offerings from the Ozarks and beyond."

"So what exactly you expect me to do?" I asked. Found myself growin' a lil impatient, truth be told. 'Tween Mister G and ol' Ray, I'd had just 'bout enough muddy-talk. "Sir," I added, thinkin' of my wages.

Mister G just kept on. "We call ourselves the Taney County Supper Club—though that title does little to illuminate our true endeavors—and tonight we hold our annual potluck. Extravagant dishes prepared by hand. The finest and most exotic ingredients these lands have to offer. Conversation and debate in which our imminent secession will be discussed. Heated, integral pontification of which so few are privy.

"And you," Mister G aimed his soppy stogie at my heart, "are going to hear and see things beyond your wildest dreams."

Now, like I say, had me enough ramblin', but they was somethin' hot-blooded in him sayin' all that while stood beneath the 'Ronny Bosch painting. I was interested. He got me, and I ain't too proud to admit it.

"Any moment now," Mister G said, "our esteemed guests will be seated, and the potluck will commence."

At that, Ray snapped-to. "Shall I make the announcement, sir?"

Mister G simply nodded.

Ray marched for the double-panel doors and give me his brightest smile on the way out.

"You," the old man kept on at me, "will stand right by that door until I say otherwise."

Otherwise, what? I wondered to myself. The hell did that mean? Reckon my brow done raised up of its own accord because Mister G waved me off.

"My contribution to the potluck requires some assistance," he said. "I am not the man I once was. At one time, I could have lifted you by the red-ear to set you on my knee. But now–"

Mister G gestured at his own self: a skel'ton wrapped in a suit.

Tell you what, even knowin' what I knowed about the swift-slide of age, I couldn't imagine Mister G was ever of a size to give a fair squeeze, let alone pick me up. But whatever, I let him believe it.

Sure, ol' timer, sure. I nodded some more.

"After you and I have made the proper

preparations, you will be free to enjoy the grounds as you see fit. The basement bar, you'll find, is stocked with all manner of libations. Or, if you prefer something of a kick," Mister G plugged one vein-streaked nostril and sniffed, "our dear Ray will provide whatever you need."

"What about the food?" I asked.

"What about it?"

"Well," I shuffled my feet, "it's getting kind of late. Ain't had nothin' since breakfast. Just wonderin' if I was able to get me a plate of them 'rare-ificated delicacies' you was on about."

Mister G eyed me like a pup, shocked to find he caught the squirrel.

"Reckon y'all might have some leftovers, it bein' a potluck and all." My gut growled. "Say, what kind of grub do you–"

"Forgive me," Mister G interrupted, "but I don't believe your palette is suitable for the flavors and textures in store." His face had gone blueish, like some old folks do when they're gettin' fussy. "Tell you what," he said, "once the table is set, I'll send Ray down to the main drag and we'll pick you up something more appropriate."

"Still got a Fuddruckers up here? Used to be one out by the Dolly Parton show when I's a boy."

"Ours is the only one left in the country," Mister G said with a little song in his throat. "Would you like that, son?"

Much as I hated for a man to talk down at me that'a'way, I'll admit a Fuddruckers burger with onion rings and a malt sounded purty good.

I imagined Mister G ate some shit like that scene in the ol' Jurassic Park. Y'all 'member that one? They's eatin' dinner with that fancy sum'bitch, and out come these big plates of piss with heaps of carrots and beans and what have you.

No thanks.

Thought maybe I ought to go ahead and put my take-out order in with Mister G, but before I opened my jaw, the doors flung wide and in come the stampede.

Five of 'em, at first, and talkin' so fast I couldn't catch who was sayin' what to who. It were like watchin' a mallard flock come up the dock of a night. Just a'chatterin' and hollerin' and honkin' tales only they could ever know. Never passin' you so much as a glance.

No intent to serve, ducks. Ain't a beast could care less for a master. 'Cept maybe cats.

Yeah, cats, too, I reckon.

I looked over to Mister G as the guests came at me. What was I supposed to do again—?

The old man just waggled his bejeweled fingers and snapped his stogie back in his mouth. "Welcome, welcome," he said. "My lovelies! My babies! My friends and favored!"

I recalled that I was to stand by the door, but as I made my way around that fat fuckin' table, this big ol' gal come right up against me.

"One side," she called, and I slumped along the wall.

She wedged past, and I stood sweatin' as the followin' four came up around to greet Mister G. I could smell pot smoke off one and seen they was all smokin' somethin' or other. Pipes and pens and nails.

The air got hot and close, and I hauled in my

gut to sneak past as quick as could be.

Seemed to me that ever' single one o' them guests turned a leg or pulled a 'bow to shove into me as I squeezed by.

"Ope!" I whispered. "Sorry," I said. "Pardon," I apologized.

Glares. Stares. Snarls.

Fuckin' rich folks, I thought. Fuckin' pieces of shit, but I just smiled and thought of my check.

Once I got through the line of guests and back to the door, I heard somethin' comin' down the hall. I could smell it, too. Loud and ripe–

–Now listen here, boys, what I'm about to say is the truth, and I don't wanna see no snickerin.' I'm serious here. You wanna hear the truth, I'm here to give it–

So anyhow, I hear this barkin.' And I smell a heap o' piss–

–Yes, like a dog. Barkin' like a dog, goddammnit–

–What? No, I said they was like ducks, not cats. Well, hell I know cats don't bark, god damn you. This ain't…Y'all ain't listenin'! Let me finish–

RELEASE THE HORSE

So I heard this barkin,' like a dog, and I sort o' tilted my head to see down the hall. And the barkin' was gettin' louder and I's hearin' this sort of shufflin' sound too.

"Detta-May! Get on in here," somebody screamed.

I turned and see that the big ol' gal from before had turned to the door.

"For God's sake," she said to Mister G, "I swear she's getting worse. The woman is dripping off the vine, Gurty.

Gurty? Was that Mister G's name? Sweet Jesus, what a gas.

Ain't had too much time to ponder the hilarity of this development on account of the shamblin' mess what come in beside me.

She was an ancient, musty, thing, and the apparent source of that urine stench. Reckon she was four-foot and a half, even. Painted up like the earth's oldest doll. Head o' steel wire, some of which was strung into little bows of faded pink and baby blues. She had no less than six sundresses on, one atop the other, till she was billowy and stranded as will'er tree.

"Hello there, young man," she said.

I took a step back on account of them milk white eyeballs and the thick gunk strung across her fake chompers.

"How do?" She asked.

"Hidy, ma'am," I said, and give a lil bow of some sort. Not sure why I done that. Nerves, 'spose.

"Come on up here, Detta-May," the big gal repeated. "You know better than to speak with the help."

I pretended like I ain't just catch a stray, and told the little ol' woman I was just fine, thank you, and asked where her dog had gone. "What's the pup's name?"

"Dog?" Detta-May replied. "Why, last time I had me a dog was before Nixon."

"Oh," I said. "I could'uh swore they was one makin' a fuss just 'fore you come in."

Somebody cleared their throat, a lil too loud for my liking.

"How about that," Detta-May answered, and

without another word, turned from me and walked away.

As she was makin' her way along the table, that godawful barkin' picked up again. Nobody else was lookin', but I realized the old woman was doin' it, by God!

Just like a damn dog, I swear it on my own Meemaw.

Well, once Detta-May took her seat beside the head o' the table, everybody else followed suit and grabbed a chair. Except for Mister G.

"Before we begin," the old man said, standin' beneath the Bosch. "I would like to thank each and every one of you for joining me tonight. Now, I won't bore you with the commencement rites this year. And no, we shan't partake in the orgasmic saturnalia of our group efforts—I believe some of us may have grown too old for such fun—" he winked at the old woman "—but we still hold true the traditions set before us by the Ozarkian Empire of old. We will feast, and we will foster, and we will give order to the wilds of our kingdom.

"Lucinda Carter," he said and pointed to that

rude ol' gal beside him. "You, the second highest contributor to our bountiful farmlands– Queen of organically produced American toils– Chieftain and Lord of in-state cannabis enterprises…What have you to offer the kin of your homeland?"

"I," Lucinda put a ring-clogged hand to her chest, "offer you The Salad of Many Stomachs."

A man of simple pleasures, I certainly am, but I ain't too proud to admit that Lucinda Carter was one mighty woman. Fact is, I don't normally spring for females if you take my meanin'. I see the beauty in a woman clear as anyone else, but beautiful women don't care for what I got to offer as much as purty men do.

And look, simple man as I am, I like to fuck purty folks.

That big ol' gal was hot stuff for sure, but she weren't never gonna turn no eyes on the help. And that weren't on the docket of wishes nor dreams for this big, dumb bear neither. You see what I'm sayin'?

If y'all think the mess at Taney Bluff come to fruit over me makin' untoward'ish moves at Miss

Fancy Salads, you're out of line.

Well, anyways, Ray come in through the doors like a bell done gone off. Had a lil white cap on his head, like the French'y chef on The Puppets Show. Ray was smilin', and he pushed a metal cart right up beside the table. He pulled a big ass bowl off the wheelie-deal and set it before the guests. It was heaped with funky lookin' greens that seemed to sparkle or catch the light.

"You will note," Lucinda said and pointed at the bowl, "that the Venus Flytrap is native to the Carolina coast." She lifted a hefty frond from the mound and held it out for all to admire.

"However," she continued, "this varietal was bred in our native soil along a specially cultivated springside humidor. With the love and care of my top geneticists, this beauty is capable of decimating our Lyme-bearing tick outbreak in an estimated four years time…But for our purposes–" she beamed "–I've devised the ultimate vehicle for an ethically sourced, pro-restorative, culinary high."

"Don't tease us, sugar," the wiry man beside her pouted. "Let's have the goods; how is Miss Lucinda gonna fuck us up this year?"

The table busted out at that one. Big laughs and fork-rattlin' table-slaps.

A stray bark.

I gave a giggle just to play a long and Lucinda Carter fixed on me with hate.

"As I was saying," she rolled her gaze back to the flytrap, "this special crop was hybridized with my High Times triple-crown winning indica: Winter's Boner Kush. This infusion has created a self-regulating trichome production unlike any other cannabis flora known to man. In fact, I believe that ninety-five percent of all hash-related products will be–"

"Looks like it's ate," said a fat-fuck like me with a pumpkin-pie haircut from across the table. "What's it got in them jaws?"

"Brandy, if you'd let me finish–" Lucinda dropped the sparkly plant back into the bowl.

"I ain't gonna eat ticks again," the big'un named Brandy cut her off. "We tried that one time. What was it they'd been sucklin' on? Was it Bald Eagle?"

"Albino cave-bat," Mister G answered. "Do go on, dear Lucinda."

RELEASE THE HORSE

"Thank you, Gurty" she said. "They aren't ticks, you titty-munching buffoon. These are ladybugs–propagated by our entomology hallucinogenicist department, of course–that have mutated over many generations to have glandular disorders which produce exorbitant amounts of dimethyltryptamine. I've had them designed to be of a violet hue and to be marked by exactly two spots on their elytra. Not that you'll get to see it. But I love a hidden aesthetic, you know. Oo," she cooed, "I've got photos from the lab if you like–" she reached for something beneath her seat "–Oh! Wait, that's not all."

Someone sighed.

"Well, it wouldn't be The Salad of Many Stomachs if it were only the two, now would it?" Lucinda snapped. "My lovely lavender ladybugs are engineered to be especially voracious in their aphid-centric appetites. As such, we have devised an experimental breed of aphidoidea which secrete an intoxicant that is striking similar to a naturally occurring–"

Now, to me, it sounded like she said them lil bugs they worked up made 'meth-dilly-Oxymethamphetamine,' but one of your boys here was kind enough to tell me that's some more muddy-talk for 'ecstasy.'

Or the MPMA.

Molly, whatever the kids call it.

"How exhilarating," Mister G said. "Payton McCullough. He wiped a bead of sweat beneath his Stetson and pointed at the thin feller beside Lucinda. "The most recent but no less esteemed member of our annual gatherings. The youngest billionaire to ever be birthed from the bloody crevice of our land. The owner and visionary behind the Ozarks' many amusement facilities and themed entertainments. Baron of the Branson Strip–"

"Bastard of the bedsheets," fat Brandy hollered. The two men seated at either side of his girth were all silence and heavy brows.

"That too, that too," Mister G agrees. "Our boy sure is a rooster! Well, what have you, Payton McCullough, to offer the kin of your homeland?"

"Funnel-Cake Fever," Payton said and snapped his fingers. He had a shit-eatin' mustache and too much makeup on for a man of his age.

Didn't care for his black bow-tie or the cut of his snappy suit. Looked like a real piece o' work to me. Just the type I expected to run all them stupid theme parks and sing-song dinner shows for old folks.

Ray took a wide plate off the cart and placed it beside Lucinda's bowl. Unlike her salad of horrors, this lil asshole looked like he brung the good stuff. Fritter-fried goodies like gold nuggets. Snowcaps of powdered sugar. A gust of heavenly oil and churned brown-butter.

"Hey," Lucinda said, staring at the plate. "You brought this last year!"

"No," Payton said, "that was Funnel-Cake Fortune. This is Funnel-Cake Fever."

"Oh, right," Brandy said. "How much cash you put in the batter for that one?"

"Ten?" Payton squinted and licked his 'stache. "Fifty? A hundred. I can't recall."

"It was seventy-five million," Lucinda offered, "and you pulled it from the ashes of industry-wide part-time benefits. I liked that one. Nice and bitter."

"Regardless," Payton said, "Funnel-Cake Fever is the tried and true recipe used throughout our various establishments…but–"

He lifted one turd-diggin' digit like a kid with the dumbest idea'r you ever heard

"–this batch has been carefully muddled with the pureed corpse of one Eugene W. Cleaver, formerly of Lebanon, Missouri."

I got real still. Felt somethin' hot at my sides. Cold near the throat-hole.

"Unfortunately for Eugene, the July heat at our Old Time Home living-museum caused the eighty-six year old performer to pass away unexpectedly. On the clock, of course, the fucking deadbeat."

Purple streaks flushed tiny Payton McCullough's cheeks, and for just a moment, I seen the vicious freak beneath all that concealer and grease.

"A lifelong member of our staff, I was able to offer Eugene's family a small fee for the remains– trailer people, you know– and thought it only right that his last performance be of the digestive persuasion. Seeing as all worms return to shit, of course."

Okay, the way you boys is lookin' at me right now–? That's exactly how I was lookin' at all o' them. I reckon y'all think I'm crazy, or stupid enough to try and take you'uns for a ride. Well, like I say, that was my reaction, too.

What in the absolute-fuck was goin' on here?

"Good show as always, Payton," Mister G said. "And now, to our longest standing legacy members–a family which lay claim to the Ozarkian Empire long before even my own–Brandy, Randy, and Tandy, our beloved and most fearsome Bandy Triplets!

"Never has a Bandy met a fish it could not hook. Nary a beast the Bandy Clan has not brought to ground. And not a single, breathing soul who could know the depths of their riches.

"Millions of fish and game licenses are acquired each year in our territory. Thousands of acres purchased and maintained for the sole purpose of the hunt. Worldwide sporting-good corporations, weapons manufacturing…All of it approved and divided by the Bandy Triplets.

"So," Mister G pointed at the three men, "Brandy," the fat-so, "Randy," a bearded, toothless idiot, "Tandy," a bespectacled oaf with dead-eyes, "What have you to offer the kin of your homeland?"

"We brung Big Bill," Brandy said. "Plank-grilled."

Ray dropped to his knees and hauled up an enormous slab of wood. It looked fit to slip from the ol' boy's hands but he plopped it on the table at the last second with a thud. His chef hat drooped to one side like a bored cock, and he readjusted it with a subtle swipe.

And there it was. A famous fish, if ever there was one. As long and thick as Mayhew's coyote.

Listen here, this'n outta be real easy to prove. I mean, it's Big Bill, man!

Flopped out, cooked, and dead—right there in front of me. Surely y'all been down to the Trout Champs Outlet and checked the damn tank!

I mean, how else you explain a forty-three pound brown trout gone missing? You think that sucker just leapt on outta there? That fuckin' fish been swimmin' around in that store since I's in school!

You gotta be shittin' me...Well are you sure it's the same fish? You weigh it out? Yes, I'm fuckin' serious, y'all better put that motherfucker on a scale and see what's what. If it's any less than forty-six big El Bees, why, that there's evidence.

Fine. Yeah. I'll keep goin'.

"A striking contribution, boys," Mister G beamed down at them three Meander-Talls like he was Papa Caveman.

I seen the two quiet ones was starin' at the dead fish. Droolin' and all that. Guess they was purty excited to chow down on Big Bill.

"Detta-May Warden," Mister G said and placed his hand on the ol' bag's shoulder. "Heiress and executor of the Warden Black Walnut estate, and dear friend to each and every one of us...What have you to offer the kin of your homeland?"

"Well, I been havin' me a hard time gettin' around these days," Detta-May said. "Can't do much of anything on my own."

Since the old woman were the only guest who

gave me the time o' day, I felt sorta sorry for her. I reckon a moneyed person like'at got maids and butlers and all kind'uh folk to help her out, but she reminded me of my poor, blessed Meemaw.

"Seein' as I couldn't go through too much trouble this year–" a single tear fell from her worn-out, ivory eyes, "–I just brung baby meats."

Ray, like a whip, slid a charred'cutie board across the dinin' table. Thin slices. Pink. Tender. Wet.

I looked around like maybe somebody would start laughin' again. Like maybe they was pullin' a funny to get me scare't. But nobody laughed. Nobody even looked to see my reaction.

Instead, Mister G snapped his fingers at Ray, and he marched back out the door pushin' his cart.

"And now," the old man said with thunder in his pipes, "the moment you've all been waiting for…"

Mister G took a beat to get the juices goin', and boys, I tell you what, you could feel it.

"Did you really catch one?" Lucinda blurted.

"Yes, yes, the rumors are true. I have indeed

captured it. It is, in fact, on its way to this very room."

"My God, Gurdy!" Lucinda declared.

"How thrilling." Payton gave his best golf-clap.

"Ain't no way," the fat Bandy shook his head.

Detta-May barked.

After all, I'd seen and heard, a lark or not, I was on my way out. I didn't care to see whatever in the living-fuck these whack-o's had planned. Screw the money. To hell with the NBA paper. I reached out and pushed open the doors–

"Why thank you, kind sir!" Ray appeared and pushed the cart right on past me. Only now, there weren't no plates or bowls or platters. Now, they was just a cage on it. And they was chains wrapped tight 'round the whole thing. And them chains was heavy.

I could tell right away somethin' were alive in there. It was rockin' around more than it should with such a careful a driver at the handle. Heard noises too. Like words, but not.

Gibberish.

Ray wedged the cart right on up the dinin' table once more and left it there. He bowed graciously to the room, nobody saw nor cared, and he walked right on outta there. Weren't long 'fore I heard the shuttle-bus turn over and wheels went crunchin' down the drive.

I didn't give nobody my Fuddruckers order, I thought. Where in the hell is he–?

Mister G coughed noisily into his withered fist. I looked up, and he was stood beside the cage. The old man reeled me in with his eyes.

I come away from the doors real slow at first, and then I seen they was all lookin' at me. Not through me no more. it was like they was seein' me for the first time.

As I come closer to the cart, that cage started thumpin' and bumpin'. I could hear them noises better, and thought I caught clarity in a babbled line of gnashin' teeth and curled lips.

"Frig you– swallow– snap it– taste red."

"Son," Mister G huffed at me. "Lift the cage for an old man. Place it on the table, if you please."

"What you got in there?" I asked, too scare't

RELEASE THE HORSE

to touch it.

"Who the hell do you think you are?" Lucinda frothed. "Listen to your superiors!"

Got me real flustered, that gal. I done what she told me and picked it up. The cage was lighter than I 'spected, but I could feel the thing inside throwin' itself around. I put it down on the table like it was pie-sonous and backed away.

"The chains, son," Mister G pointed. "Open'er up for us. Now."

I'm tellin' y'all right now: I don't know why I did it. I don't know what come over me. I ain't a man what lets nobody do me the way them folks was goin' at it. It ain't in my nature.

But I did it. I undid the twist-lock and pulled off them chains. Put my sweaty thumb on the latch and flipped it. Heard the thing inside go quiet as I lifted the hatch.

And there it was.

Whatever it was.

"The Woolybugger," Mister G announced.

Like I say, my dearest Meemaw had plenty of

lil sayings and words for things that folks forgot to name. Funny stuff, usually. But spooky shit, too.

Any of y'alls Meemaws warn on the dangers of fishin' near a Gollywog's hole? Or how the Jimpicule might come to follow ye on the nightly stroll? Well, mine did.

And she also told me about them Woolybuggers. Said they used to be ever'where you looked down in the caves near her home. Told me nowadays, you only see 'em humpin' across the backroads come late of a night; that you could only spy one if you was alone or with your lover.

They'd dash out a'fore your foglights, she said, and you'd think you seen the biggest caterpillar they ever was. But really, it were a warm-blooded beast. Mammalian'ated, even. Like a pole-cat with ten hundred lil paws and a spine that rolled easy as jelly. Spike-tipped furs of a porcupine and the cowardice of an opossum.

Ornery buggers, she'd say.

Well, what slithered outta that cage sure didn't look ill-tempered to me. Pitiful, I'd call it. About six foot long but only as wide as your average wood-weasel.

Everything else my Meemaw said was about right. 'Cept all them stumpy legs didn't end in no paws. They was lil feet and hands. I could see dark nails like a raccoon's on each and ever' one of 'em, too.

It was awful weak comin' outta that cage. I figured it plum wore out after all that carryin' on. Probably hurt itself against the walls. Held its head down low, like it was ashamed to be seen.

"Holy rollin' shitter-on-fire," Brandy said. He reached out and tore a chunk outta Big Bill's belly and stuffed it in his mouth. "That's a damn woofy-fuffer," he said between bites.

"Yessir'ee. A genuine Ozarkian mystery plumbed from the depths of the grand caverns beneath us. Lord knows how many men I sent down into that hole. Only a few ever come back. Only one returned with this feller here. Wasn't much left of him, but he did it. God rest his soul."

"Is it sick?" Lucinda asked.

"Starved," Mister G replied. "Hasn't had a scrap since the day it tore our poor spelunkers to pieces. My great, great, great Gram'papa told me a Woolybugger don't taste like nothing lest you give 'em a good meal right before you take it to slaughter."

"Well, I've brung plenty of baby," Detta-May whined. "Do you think your Woolybugger likes baby-meats?"

"Why, that's mighty kind of you Detta-May." Mister G picked at a sullied bow in her hair. "But fortunately, I've already meal-prepped. You can save those sweet meats for finer tongues, my dear."

It was 'round this time that the three ape-brothers got out their seats and come over to me. I thought they was comin' to help grab whatever Mister G was plannin' to feed the thing–

Randy and Tandy each took one o' my arms. Brandy got behind me and pressed somethin' hard to my back. Reckon y'all know what it was.

"Move, and I'll shoot," the tubby-fucker whispered.

"Well, son," Mister G moved in on me, "this has been a pleasure, I'm sure. But we're all hankering for a meal. Especially our new compadre. And really, what else are you good for?"

Tandy and Randy bent me at the waist and slammed my face against the dinin' table. The Woolybugger slithered around my dome and started crawlin'. As it came near, it reared back on two hundred legs, give or take, and I seen its face.

Kinda looked like Detta-May. Or one o' her dead babes. A sad, puckered feller. Grey and wise. Scare't and alone. I could hear it murmerin' at me as it came in closer. Soft words. Clear as day.

I looked up at the ol' Ronny Bosch painting and said my peace. The critters and scallywags all over his work, his achievement, they reminded me of the Woolybugger. Wild doo-dads, like innocent children of God…Just lil dudes, you know?

And then the screaming.

So loud. Desperate. Agita'lated.

Figured I was dead. Floatin' down the river of Hades, most likely. All was lost, and so was I.

Warmth and wetness sloshed my face. I looked across the table and it was red. The Woolybugger was gone and there weren't nobody holdin' me down. Fact was, two arms lay beside my feet. I looked around the room, and blood covered the walls. A strip o' stomach dangled from the corner of the Ronny Bosch like a snake on a sill.

They was a slurpin' sound comin' down wind, so I turned to look.

Against one wall, the Woolybugger was stood up, straight as a pole. Mister G—half of him—stuck out it's wide mouth.

Never knew a pair of jaws could get that big. Never seen a critter so stuffed. Never seen a man so afraid to die.

"Long live the Ozarki—" he started to shout.

The Woolybugger zipped him straight down its throat. Snapped its mouth shut. Burped and blew. Mister G's Stetson parachuted down to the floor.

So that's it, boys.

That's the whole story.

Right after that, I turned and I flew. Straight out the doors and down off the bluff. Come straight to y'all. Flagged down the first pig I seen on the Strip. Took you boys up to the house. Gave it all.

So what now? You talk to my boss, Blevins?

RELEASE THE HORSE

You find Ray?

—bodies?

Bodies?

Look, y'all want them bones. I got a cave and about six foot of rope to give ye. And that's it. That's all I got.

You can take me at my word or not at all.

ACKNOWLEDGEMENTS

THE BAND originally appeared in In *The Shadow of the Horns: A Black Metal Horror Anthology* from Castaigne Publishing (OOP)

LITTLE MAN originally appeared in the October 2022 issue of Pyre Magazine (Online Only)

THE FAMILY WHISTLE originally appeared in 206 Word Stories from Bag of Bones Press (Charity Antho)

RELEASE THE HORSE originally appeared in *Hellarkey II* from Malarkey Books (OOP)

Matthew Mitchell is a fiction and comics writer from the Ozarks. His award-winning novella *Chaindevils* was published by Weirdpunk Books, and his short fiction has appeared in anthologies from Castaigne Publishing, Filthy Loot Press, and various others. Matthew's comics have appeared in *Heavy Metal Magazine* and he is co-editor of the *Horrorium* comics anthology.

FILTHY LOOT
"MISFIT FICTIONS"
AMES IA | EST. 2019

FILTHY LOOT is an independent press, based out of Ames, IA. Focused on misfit fictions and odd other ideas — we publish books, zines and assorted miscellany in both open and limited edition formats.

HORROR/WEIRD FICTION TITLES
- ☐ *Gone to Seed* by Justin Lutz
- ☐ *Hairs* by S.T. Cartledge
- ☐ *Hollow Coin* by S.T. Cartledge
- ☐ *Kayfabe* by Madison McSweeney
- ☐ *Pacifier* by Ira Rat
- ☐ *Participation Trophy* by Ira Rat
- ☐ *Shagging the Boss* by Rebecca Rowland
- ☐ *Strange Spells* by Edwin Callihan
- ☐ *The Doom that Came To Mellonville* by Madison McSweeney
- ☐ *The God in the Hills and Other Horrors* by Jon Steffens
- ☐ *The God in the Hills 2: Abhorrent Flesh* by Jon Steffens
- ☐ *The Vine that Ate the Starlet* by Madeleine Swann
- ☐ *Wax and Wane* by Saoirse Ní Chiaragáin

HORROR/WEIRD FICTION ANTHOLOGIES
- ☐ *BodyPunk*
- ☐ *Dirt in the Sky*
- ☐ *Fucked Up Stories to Read in the Daytime*
- ☐ *Isolation is Safety*
- ☐ *LAZERMALL*
- ☐ *Psycho Teenage Freak-Out*
- ☐ *Teenage Grave*
- ☐ *Teenage Grave 2*
- ☐ *Soft Ceremonies*

www.ingramcontent.com/pod-product-compliance
Lightning Source LLC
LaVergne TN
LVHW031611060526
838201LV00065B/4814